The Persian Waltz

JOHNNY

ACKNOWLEDGMENTS

A big thank you:

To Caroline Ciaglia for her invaluable help with editing.
To Chris Kozak for his advice and critical eye.

Thanks also to:

Maggie Mortenson and John Hoffman for their support and encouragement. It is invaluable.
Cici and John Welsh, for being the first to read and give me feedback.
Steve Gray for his insights and counsel and for having a really cool wife in Nancy
Irene Graham for showing me the way and inspiring me.
Finally, thank you Andy Gutowski for your fantastic work on the cover.

JOHNNY

To my parents, Tom and Noreene,

CHAPTER 1

He needed a happy distraction, something to take his mind off work. It was Friday afternoon and the *Prater*, Vienna's famous amusement park, was the popular place to be. Billy Mack sat in the *Prater's* beer garden and let the sun warm his face as he watched the waves of people stroll by. He smiled each time he saw someone laughing or a young couple holding hands.

His full-figured waitress returned with his beer and set it on the table next to his iPhone. She wore the traditional Austrian Dirndl, a green dress and red apron over a low-cut white blouse. He thanked her, took a healthy sip of beer and turned his attention back to the smiles and laughs. He thought of life's priorities as wide-eyed children skipped past heading to the bumper cars, the spinning teacups or any ride with a blinking light. Parents followed, keeping their kids within sight and yelling at those who strayed too far.

High above him, the iconic Ferris wheel known as *The Wiener Riesenrad* leisurely rotated its wooden red gondolas. The vintage square gondolas reminded Mack of the scene in the classic movie *The Third Man* in which Orson Wells moved elusively inside one of the gondolas while lecturing Joseph Cotton on the insignificance of human life in post-World War II Vienna. Mack imagined living in war-torn Vienna in 1946, a dangerous asylum with an underbelly of wayward soldiers, ruthless spies, con men and cold-blooded killers — where you survived on your guts and your guile.

A ringing cell phone from a nearby table shook him back to the here and now, to the peaceful, neutral Vienna with its buildings hovering over the park. He lifted his beer to the tranquil skyline and took a long, slow sip, unaware of the new dangerous underbelly now lurking in the city.

William McMillan, or 'Billy Mack' to his friends, just finished two arduous weeks of working eighteen-hour days with barely enough sleep to stay functional. He was leading a multi-billion dollar corporate takeover with a deadline to close the deal five days away. Earlier in the day, final negotiations hit a snag and the opposing parties agreed to a much-needed two-day cooling-off period. Tomorrow Mack planned to travel a half hour south to the town of Bad Vöslau to spend a restful weekend with friends. He was looking forward to some home cooking, a collector's wine cellar and two days with no demands on his time.

Priorities.

Picking up his phone, he examined the device tethering him to his office. Most of his friends won't walk out their front door without their phone in hand and can't go thirty-seconds without checking the screen. *Lost touch to a touch screen*, he thought and smiled. He was just as guilty. He always had his phone with him and checked it all too often. He claimed he had an excuse: His boss required him to carry the newest iPhone with him *twenty-four seven*. Looking for any reason to turn off his phone, he read the time on his watch as *twenty-five eight* and eagerly powered down the device. He stuck it in his blue blazer and resumed his people watching. Ahead of him was a busy evening of doing nothing.

Priorities.

In the walkway, a few meters from his table, a small blonde-haired girl squatted on her haunches and cried as her eyes darted back and forth from the scoop of chocolate ice cream lying on the asphalt to the empty wafer cone in her hand. As she reached for the melting ball of chocolate, her exasperated mother ran over and slapped her little hand. She scolded her in Russian then yanked her by the arm and pulled her toward the ice cream stand.

In the middle of the walkway, a stunning woman with thick, black hair and aviator sunglasses came to a sudden stop in order to avoid being run over by the mother and the young girl. She removed her sunglasses and smiled fleetingly at the little girl as she was dragged past.

The olive-skinned beauty scanned the beer garden until she made eye contact with Mack. Keeping her gaze fixed on him, she glided down the walkway until she came to a stop directly in front of his table. Looking down at him, her coffee-brown eyes contemplated her next move.

Mack was captivated. As a former Major League baseball player, Mack was used to women approaching him out of the blue. During his playing days he could instantly tell what a woman wanted by the way she looked at him. He looked up at the face of the exotic woman staring down at him and he had no idea what she wanted. It was a new feeling.

The waitress reappeared, interrupting the staring contest. *"Was Wünschen Sie?"* she asked, grinned at the woman and waited.

As soon as the woman shifted her eyes to the waitress, Mack sat up and self-consciously ran his fingers through his wavy brown hair. Like most ex-pro athletes, he'd kept himself in good shape. He was very disciplined, running five miles every other morning and practicing Taekwondo on the days in-between. A woman he recently dated described him as *muscularly thin*. He didn't know what it meant exactly but liked the description. Regrettably, on this trip to Vienna his workout routine had been interrupted by work.

The mysterious woman took her time answering and the waitress switched to English, asking, "What would you like?"

"I would like a green tea with lemon, please," the woman replied in fluent German with a Viennese dialect.

The red-faced waitress nodded and quickly disappeared behind the crowd gathered near a pretzel vendor.

"I am Siva," the woman said and covertly glanced over her shoulder. Seemingly satisfied with what she saw or didn't see, she sat down. "I know you don't have much time..."

"Excuse me?"

"Follow my lead." Siva leaned in and kissed Mack on each cheek as if they were more than friends.

Mack felt her body press against his and her right hand caress his back. He inhaled her seductive perfume of lilac, jasmine and vanilla, triggering an image in his mind that had nothing to do with the gondola scene in *The Third Man.*

Siva's left hand gently stroked his cheek as she whispered in his ear, "I am being followed. Put your arm around my shoulder like we are in love." Mack followed her orders and she snuggled into him. He pulled her close. Her lips brushed his ear and she softly said, "I hope you are smiling because the men who are following me just walked by. I don't think they saw us." A sudden gust of wind blew her shiny black hair across her face. She easily hooked it behind her ear and settled her brown eyes back on Mack.

"We don't have much time," Siva said with urgency. "My contact has promised the final delivery tomorrow. It's the most important piece of evidence so you must be very careful. It is confirmed General Farid is leading the operation and is in Vienna. That means the Ayatollah has given his approval." Without moving her head, Siva's eyes scanned the park. "I'll meet you here tomorrow with the final package, same time."

She pulled away. "I must go before those men come back. Please take the appropriate precautions when you leave. The men who walked by are Jahangir." She pronounced it *Ya-hahn-jeer.* "There is a team of Jahangir in Vienna led by the two brothers who just walked by. You must stop them while they are here. If even one of these terrorists is able to leave Vienna, it will end in disaster. Tomorrow we learn the identities of the others. Until then, stay vigilant."

Siva kissed Mack, letting her lips linger on his, then stroked his cheek. She was a brilliant actress. Mack was nearly convinced they were lovers. After a furtive check of the surroundings, Siva stood and looked down at him with a combination of hope and fear. A second later, she turned and slipped into a wave of people heading toward the ice cream stand.

CHAPTER 2

Mack took a slow, distracted swig of his beer as his eyes followed Siva down the walkway. It didn't take him long to decide what he should do. He wiped his mouth with his sleeve, stuck a twenty Euro note under his glass to pay for his half-finished beer and for Siva's still-to-be-delivered green tea then hurried after her. A hundred meters past the crowd gathered at the ice cream stand, Siva turned left into the main plaza and headed toward the front gate. Breaking into a jog, Mack rounded the corner to see Siva standing stock still only a few meters from the park's main gate. Two dark-skinned men sporting trimmed beards and dressed in identical leather jackets were approaching her with cautious determination. The man Mack took to be in charge was shaking his finger at Siva while the other, more cautious man held his right hand inside his coat and was moving around Siva. When they reached her, each man gripped an elbow and steered her away from the main entrance. Siva twisted and turned squirming to free her arms. As she struggled to get away, she screamed, "Let me go," then switched to German and yelled, *"Hilfe! Hilfe!"*

The people standing in the main plaza looked over at the commotion and either averted their eyes or quickly moved in the opposite direction acting as if nothing was happening.

Mack broke into a sprint. Three meters from the man who had his right hand inside his jacket, he lowered his shoulder as if he were colliding with the catcher at home plate. Barely missing Siva, he drove his shoulder underneath the man's rib cage and exploded his forearms out as he came up. The man flew backward, fell hard and cracked his head against a thick concrete wall. The eerie crack of a cervical vertebrae snapping in half echoed off the cement and his body went limp. From the crooked angle of his head, his neck was clearly broken. Lying next to his limp right hand was a nine-millimeter Glock.

Mack paid no attention to the dead man. He'd kept his balance and rapidly spun three hundred sixty degrees whipping his right heel up and around striking the other man in the side of the head. The man was so traumatized by his partner lying lifeless on the ground he didn't react to the kick. Siva flinched at the loud thud of Mack's heel thumping the man's cheekbone.

The bearded man's knees wobbled and his eyes

rolled back into his head. He dropped to his knees, teetered, then fell forward landing face first on the chest of the dead man.

Mack rolled him over and realized the two men were identical twins. One was breathing and the other was not. He snatched the dead man's pistol off the asphalt, grabbed Siva by the hand and hurried them out the gate.

Siva ran to a taxi parked directly outside the front entrance, her hands were shaking. Mack pocketed the pistol, glanced back at the two men then ran after Siva, keeping an eye out for police.

"Do not say a word inside the taxi," Siva said, her words running together. "We act like nothing happened." Unable to stop her trembling, she hugged Mack in an effort to calm herself and catch her breath.

"Where did you learn to do that?"

"Baseball and Taekwondo."

She looked at him strangely.

Keeping a secure grip on the pistol in his pocket, Mack opened the taxi door and followed Siva into the backseat.

"Hegelgasse Neun," Siva said to the driver, giving him the destination address.

The stocky, leather-faced driver nodded and straightened this thinning gray hair. The picture on the taxi permit was of a much younger, bearded man named Yusef Qasim.

For the next twenty minutes, they rode in silence through Vienna's Friday evening rush hour traffic. The driver cut across the historic *Erste Bezirk*, the Baroque, tourist-filled city center.

For the entire trip, the taxi driver couldn't stop glancing in the rearview mirror. When his attention was diverted to Siva, he nearly hit another taxi and a tram. Crossing the *Stephansplatz* in the city center, he missed hitting an elderly couple by only inches.

As the taxi approached the destination, Siva insisted on paying. She handed the driver a fifty Euro note and said, *"Dreissig ist gut."* She exited the cab and waited for her change. The driver handed her a twenty and said something derogatory in Persian.

Mack didn't understand what was said but stepped to the driver's window when he heard the man's tone.

The driver gunned the engine. "Fucking to America," he yelled out the window as he sped down the street.

"What did he say to you?" Mack asked.

"It is not important." Siva said, her face flush.

"It is to me."

After a long, calming breath, she said, "He called me a Shia whore and said I wouldn't satisfy a real man. He spoke in Persian but his accent told me he was from Kurdistan."

"I'm sorry. Don't let his ignorant words get to you."

"I don't. I am only embarrassed for my people. I learned many years ago that too many Middle Eastern men consider woman only as property to do with as they see fit."

Mack thought of the two men who attacked her.

Siva said, "I'm not Shia or even Arabic. My father was Irish and my mother was Persian. She converted to Catholicism long before she married my father."

Siva had nothing more to add and self-consciously waited for Mack to respond to her unique lineage.

Mack was only paying fleeting attention. As he perused the neighborhood, he was thinking about the man whose neck he broke.

Every city block in this older section of Vienna was dominated by large six-story stone buildings each with a main entrance consisting of double wooden doors arched at the top and wide enough to drive a horse and buggy through. Cut into each double doors was a regular-sized door with modern locks.

The street was empty and the building windows were dark. The setting sun reflected off the copper-tinted windows of the hotel at the end of the block and illuminated the entire street in an eerie, jaundiced yellow. Mack shifted his concentration down the block to a man in an overcoat loitering outside the hotel door, smoking a cigarette.

Siva stepped into his field of vision. "Thank you for what you did."

Keeping one eye on the man outside the hotel, he said, "We should talk about what just happened."

"You do not need to worry about those men. Nothing will be reported. The men who attacked me were Jahangir. I can assure you everything will be taken care of at the highest levels." Siva waited until the taxi was out of sight, then took Mack by the elbow. They crossed the street and walked one block to a rust colored stone building with a blue number six above the double wooden door.

The man smoking outside the hotel, crushed out his cigarette with his heel, stared too long at Siva then disappeared inside the hotel.

"What did those men want from you?" Mack asked.

"I don't know. I've never seen those two before."

Siva slid her key into the regular sized door cut into the larger double door. She cracked open the door and peeked inside before pushing the door open. The old building's entryway was dimly lit by a bare light bulb hanging on a wire. She stepped inside, pressed the button for the stairway lights and turned back with a cautious smile on her lips. She said, "I will see you tomorrow William, same time, same place." The door clicked shut leaving him alone on the wide sidewalk.

Mack took two steps and froze.

"How did she know my name?"

CHAPTER 3

Two blocks down the street, Mack stopped in front of an Australian-themed pub. Why did she call him William? The only person in this world who called him William was his mother. He questioned whether he should go back and confront Siva. He stared through the pub's window as if he would find the answer inside. A small crowd near the jukebox danced to Midnight Oil's *Beds are Burning*. The dancers surrendered to the thumping music as they moved around the dance floor, oblivious to the world around them.

Fighting his impulse to turn around and head back, Mack gave in to prudence and common sense, decided to collect his thoughts and determine what other questions he wanted answered before he confronted her.

Approaching the street corner, he heard a footstep and spun around. There was no one in sight and nothing moving on the street. Blaming paranoia, he still quickened his pace and took the next right. After turning the corner, he slowed and followed a skinny man walking his Doberman. At the next corner, Mack did a three-sixty spin then turned left. Thirty meters down the street he realized the entire block was dark and there was not a single person in sight. He turned and looked back. The man walking the Doberman had disappeared. Except for the sound of canned laughter coming from a television set in one of the open windows high above the street, it was strangely quiet. It was like the entire neighborhood was hiding, silently listening to the lone television. He felt like he was in an episode of the Twilight Zone.

Mack hunched his shoulders and headed in the direction of his hotel. Staying close to the curb, he heard a car engine coming up behind him. He kept his eyes forward. The car settled into Mack's pace and stayed twenty meters behind. Slipping his hand in his pocket, he gripped the Glock.

Just ahead, the door to an old stone building flew open. A broad-shouldered man in a leather sport coat stepped over the doorframe and held the door handle as he spun around. Mack readied the Glock in his pocket. As the man turned, the smile disappeared from his face.

"*Es tut Mir leid*," he said to Mack then reached back and held out his hand. A tall, leggy blonde took the man's hand and stepped over the doorframe. For an awkward moment, the couple stared at him. Finally, they said, "Schöne Abend," in unison and walked away.

By this time, the car following him had come to a stop on the street next to him. Its engine rattled like it was about to die. Mack turned to see the taxi driver looking at him like a con man eyeing his mark.

"Mr. Fucking to America, you want ride?" He asked with a smart-ass smirk.

Mack stepped off the curb and approached the driver's window. His hand gripped the Glock in his pocket a little tighter.

"Please Mr. John Wayne not to shoot me," the driver said. He grinned widely and held up his hands in mock surrender.

"I should shoot you for what you said to the woman."

The grin vanished from the taxi driver's face. "I think she was to have sex with you for money. When she go inside alone, I know I have mistake. A thousand apologies to you."

Putting his hand on the car, Mack leaned down and looked around the front seat. A copy of **Kurier**, Vienna's largest daily newspaper lay on the passenger's seat. Underneath the newspaper was a thick, dog-eared file folder.

"I give you ride. You no pay. Please for me to say to you sorry."

Mack didn't know how to react. Part of him said to walk away while another part of him said to shoot the man in the leg.

"No thank you, I'm only a couple blocks from my

hotel and want some air before I sleep."

The taxi driver held out his business card. "When you need taxi, please to call. I give special fare. I can be very helping while you here."

Mack took the card and placed it carefully in his pocket. "I can call you anytime?"

"I may have other job but if you call to me, I come for you right away. Okay Mr. John Wayne?"

The taxi driver drove down the street keeping an eye on Mack in his side mirror. Grinding the gears as he turned the corner, he gunned the engine and vanished.

Mack pulled the card out of his pocket. It only had the word *TAXI* in the center and a local phone number below.

Crisscrossing the streets until he made his way to the Ring Road, the main road circling the city center, Mack hastened his pace. Along the busy Ring Road, he stayed near the parked cars lining the narrow frontage road, looking over his shoulder every thirty feet. Where the road curved, he sprinted across the five-lanes and jogged a half block to his hotel. He stood underneath the glass overhang at Hotel Imperial's entrance and perused the busy street to see if he was followed.

The doorman was visibly uncomfortable with Mack standing in front of the entrance. Guests at Hotel Imperial do not loiter in front of the hotel. They are either coming from or going to their limousines. They are busy people, too busy to waste time looking around. Loitering is what vagrants do. When the doorman moved to approach him, Mack turned on his heel and pushed through the revolving door.

He cautiously entered his executive suite and did a cursory check of the large sitting room and the bedroom. Checking for bugs, he found the Renaissance furniture too heavy to move. The suite was more than he needed. He had no idea what the room cost. The room was booked for him and the bill was sent directly to his company, Baxter, Israel & Gunn, or as the firm was nicknamed by Wall Street, BIG.

Removing his navy blazer, Mack felt an object in the side pocket. He pulled out a black USB device and stared at it. How did this get into his pocket?

A whiff of lilac, jasmine and a touch of vanilla floated through the air. Siva must have slipped it in his pocket when she hugged him.

He opened his computer, hesitated as he held the USB device in front of his face then said, "Gotta do whatcha gotta do" and connected the device to the port.

His screen went black and the computer went into hyperdrive. The hard drive slowed as rows of pictures emerged on the screen. In the bottom right, two video icons appeared.

Mack clicked through the pictures. The dusty roads, arid hills, clay homes and numerous minarets indicated the photos were taken somewhere in the Middle East. The architecture was unmistakable. Halfway through the pictures, people began to emerge as the photo's main subject. The last two rows of pictures were from inside a high-tech manufacturing facility. In those pictures, an olive-skinned beauty with a decorative headscarf was leading a group of men as if she were giving a tour. Close to her was an overweight, bearded man in a black and white robe and white turban (the most holy color). It took a few seconds to recognize the leader of Iran. In each picture, he pointed in a different direction with a devoted look of admiration. Behind him was a group of chubby men wearing gray robes and black turbans. The woman in the pictures never smiled and in certain photos looked pained. She drew Mack's attention and it wasn't because of her beauty.

He clicked on the video icons and watched two short videos. The videos were narrated in Persian by a woman and were filmed in two separate, sophisticated manufacturing facilities. In both videos, the same woman led the group of chubby, bearded men as they strolled through the facilities admiring what they saw. The Ayatollah, still wearing the white turban was the only person dressed in his robe. The other men had changed into western-style business suits. The woman leading the group had a familiar gait. He didn't know why he focused on her striding ahead of the group, gliding to a stop to let the group of slow moving men catch up and then speaking in curt sentences, always with her eyes averted.

The first video ended with still photographs of rows and rows of metal tubes with a myriad of small pipes and wires connecting the tubes. In the final photograph, the narrator's words were clipped and wooden. After considerable pause, her last words were spoken clearly and concisely and repeated for emphasis. It seemed to Mack the language spoken in the video had an American accent.

The ending of the second video was narrated in English with Persian subtitles. It was slickly produced, as if it came from Madison Avenue. Flashing across the screen were images of the Ayatollah of Iran giving speeches followed by scenes of nuclear explosions and intense street battles with American soldiers in Iraq and Afghanistan. It ended with an animated Phoenix rising from ashes and flames. The narrator said, "*The dead in the graves will rise up and exchange places with the heretics and the traitors and destroy the world in a final battle. On the Last Day, Allah will punish the impure bloodlines, the feminists, the promiscuous, the homosexuals and the followers of all false beliefs. Out of the ashes our Supreme Leader will rise up and create a new world order under Sharia Law where the family is restored, wives submit to husbands in all matters and the impure are stoned. It is Allah's will.*" The video ended with the Iranian flag waiving from a flagpole atop the White House.

Mack tried to copy the photos and videos on to his computer. Each time he tried, an error message written in Persian or Arabic script popped up.

He called the concierge desk and asked if the hotel could provide a new USB storage device. In less than a minute there was a soft knock on his door. He clicked on the room's security video screen providing a view of the hallway and saw a woman in a black jacket and skirt standing at his door and smiling up at the camera.

He opened the door halfway.

She handed him a small paper bag folded at the top, stepped closer to the door and asked if there was anything else she could do for him. Her smile was mischievous.

Mack's attention was occupied with the paper bag

in his hand. "Thank you Karin," he said and dismissed her with a twenty Euro tip.

On the small screen he glimpsed at her walking away and didn't see the frown that had replaced her smile.

He stuck the new USB stick in an adjacent port and tried to drop and drag. The same error message appeared.

Turning his iPhone back on, he had three missed calls from Sam Baxter, his boss and the owner of BIG. That was a bad sign. One missed call was fine. Two was explainable. Three was a problem.

Returning Baxter's calls though would have to wait. Mack never talked to Sam Baxter unless he was totally prepared. He scrolled through his contacts and called Nimesh, an independent contractor to BIG and the world's leading electronic and cyber security expert. Considered the world's top hacker, no one knew Nimesh's last name or if he even had one. He'd erased his existence from every database.

Mack explained to Nimesh what he discovered on the USB device and how it came into his possession.

After scolding Mack for putting his computer at risk by inserting the USB device, Nimesh checked the computer and USB device for any malware. After confirming both devices were clean, he ran a systems sweep on Mack's computer and then taught Mack how to check the USB device for any embedded data. When a series of coded messages appeared, Mack felt like a hacker.

"What are these?" Mack asked. "A random string of numbers, letters and symbols must have some purpose."

"I don't know ... yet. Give me time to take a look," Nimesh replied. The cursor on Mack's computer ping-ponged around the screen while programs came and went at lightning speed. "Sorry, Mack, the device is 'read only' and it's protected with a sophisticated encryption. I've made a screen shot of the strings of data from the device and will start my analysis."

He thanked Nimesh and called his boss's cell phone. Rose Mueller, Baxter's secretary answered. Baxter was old school and still called her his secretary. He treated Rose the same as he treated his partners and paid her so well she didn't dare make a stink.

"Hi Rose, is Mr. Baxter available? It's--"

"Hello Mr. McMillan," Rose said, interrupting him. During business hours she was the consummate professional addressing everyone as either Mr. or Ms. "He's in a meeting and can't be disturbed. Leave your phone on and he'll call you back." It was a bad omen that Rose knew his phone had been turned off.

He tossed the phone on sofa and stretched. The image of Siva walking toward him at *Prater* came to mind. It was not an image you forget. There was a confidence and a conviction in her stride. Why then, before she walked away, did she look at him with a mixture of hope and fear?

It was the hope in her eyes that troubled him.

CHAPTER 4

General Hafez Farid was trained like all good soldiers to obey the orders from his superiors, even if the person giving the orders was an inferior human being. He meandered around the living quarters of the safe house with his cellphone stuck to his ear listening to an inferior mind lecture him and criticize his leadership.

An expanding scowl and a crimson hue grew on his face. This wasn't the first time he'd been dressed down for someone else's mistake. He could handle that. It gnawed at him that the person on the other end of the line was an incompetent Westerner who was once a Christian, more precisely a Catholic. He could handle that as well. What he couldn't handle was the humiliation of being lectured to and insulted by a woman, a woman who didn't know her place.

Finally, the woman on the other end of the line stopped talking.

"I have both men with me here," the General said in English. "They explained what happened and the problem will be resolved." General Farid did not agree with the mission's command structure but was under direct orders from the Ayatollah to take orders from this heretic. He was being forced to use all his cunning and deceit to conduct the mission his way.

"Do not forget the, um, business plan is still on target," the General said trying to remember the English code words to use in case the call was being bugged. "We have met our milestones and the delivery date is still good. The shipping company has promised us a valid quote in the next couple days. There is only the one wrinkle left to iron out and that is being taken care of."

The General had a strong bearing and an athletic build. His black hair was cropped close on the sides and thick on top. His black eyes could pierce an armored tank. Always on edge, his way of resolving problems was to kill the person responsible.

General Farid had a hair trigger of a temper but was enough of a politician to know when to keep his cool. At this moment, he would quietly tolerate the reprimand he was enduring from the woman but he would never accept it.

As he paced the floor, the General kept one eye on the two Jahangir soldiers, Tariq and Rez, sitting on the sofa. He had thought Tariq and Rez were thoroughly vetted and understood he was giving the orders.

Apparently, he was wrong about them.

"Yes," the General repeated into the phone, rolling his eyes. "If the product is not compromised, I will retrieve the device before it gets in the wrong hands. You have told me of the its importance three times. The mission will go smoothly from here on out. You have my word."

The General hung up the phone, glared at Tariq and Rez and began to shake in rage. He cocked his arm and hurled the phone at their heads. Plastic shattered as the phone hit the wall above them. Before the pieces hit the floor, General Farid had his service pistol raised and shot Rez between the eyes. Rez's head snapped back, bounced off the wall and fell onto Tariq's shoulder.

"That is the punishment for betrayal."

Tariq sat frozen waiting for the General to shoot him. He prayed, "I bear witness that there is no god but Allah."

"Do not worry, Tariq," the General said in Persian. "I am not going to kill you ... unless you betray me as well." He returned his pistol to his holster. "You and your brother were given a simple task, bring me the woman for interrogation. Instead, a woman and a Christian heretic bested you. What is worse, you let a Christian heretic kill your brother. It tells me you are a weak man, Tariq, a weak man."

General Farid had recommended the Jahangir for this mission. The Jahangir, a secret subset within Al Qaeda, was funded and controlled by Iran's Guardian Council of the Constitution. All Jahangir fighters were closely vetted and were highly trained assassins. Those selected into the Jahangir were predominantly psychopaths who thrived on killing. The Jahangir jihadists measured their loyalty on how often they were allowed to kill in the name of Allah.

Tariq pushed Rez off him and wiped the blood spatter from his face. "We were not aware this woman was meeting with a new agent, a trained assassin. I will find and kill them both by tomorrow. Praise be to Allah."

The General's mission was now down by two men, Rez and Tariq's brother Taher, and he didn't have time for any replacements to be sent from the Jahangir training camp in Libya. If the remaining Jahangir followed his orders without fail, the mission would be a success.

General Farid leaned in, nose to nose with Tariq. "You will kill no one. Find the woman and bring her to me, unharmed. If she has left Vienna, I will hold you personally responsible."

"Yes, fine," Tariq said, with an air of defiance. This was not what he signed up for. He did not volunteer for this mission so he could baby sit a heretic, and worse, a woman. "It is my duty to kill the Satan, the American assassin who killed my brother. I am owed revenge."

"You are owed what I say you are owed," the General said, his blood surging. He lit a cigarette to calm himself and exhaled the smoke in Tariq's face. "Do you even know what this American Satan looks like?"

Tariq could only shake his head, averting his eyes.

The General handed him a picture of Mack. "This is the man who killed your brother and easily knocked you out. His name is William McMillan but is called Billy Mack. You are to find where he is staying and let me know. This Billy Mack is not to know we are looking for him. Once you locate him, I will arrange for a team of experts to coerce him into telling us what I want to know. These are your orders. After our mission is successful, you can exact your revenge, not before. If you fail or do not follow my orders, I will behead you in front of your family."

General Farid kicked Rez in the head to assure he was dead. The informant's tip he received on Rez was weak but he was not one to take any chances. The Caliphate was too great to take any risk. "Take this traitor and dump the body where no one will find it."

Tariq came back into the room with a large suitcase and crammed Rez inside. As he zipped the case closed he wondered how Rez betrayed the General. Rez was the most devout of all the Jahangir soldiers. Every penny Rez earned was sent to his family near Kandahar, Afghanistan. Rez could recite the Koran by memory and talked longingly about the great Caliphate to come. Tariq secured the straps of the suitcase and dragged it to the door. How did Rez betray General Farid? This was not the right time to raise that question with the General.

Tariq lugged the suitcase out to the Ford Transit Courier van parked behind the house. He struggled to lift Rez's body into the back of the van, twice dropping the suitcase onto the driveway. He called a former university classmate who worked construction in Vienna and was sympathetic to Al Qaeda and the Jahangir. Ten minutes later, he met his university friend outside the locked gates of a large construction site. Together they dumped Rez's body into a deep hole that would be filled with concrete in the morning.

Tariq arrived back at the safe house to find Faruk, a Jahangir foot soldier from Saudi Arabia, cleaning up the blood splatter on the wall and floor. Faruk's long black hair and thick black beard were disheveled.

"Where is Rez?" Faruk asked. "He should be here helping us clean up."

"He received new orders from the General," Tariq said. "I am going out to the back to smoke before I leave."

CHAPTER 5

Mack stood on the balcony looking over the historic city of Vienna stretching out as far as the eye could see. Off in the distance, the lights of the red gondolas on the *Prater* Ferris wheel were clearly visible. In the street below, Friday night festivities in Vienna, a city of roughly two million people, reverberated up from the asphalt.

Siva's fragrance lingered on his clothes — lilacs, jasmine and a touch of vanilla. The vivid image of her walking toward the *Biergarten* came back to him. And so did the question: *How did she know his name?*

Waiting for Sam Baxter to return his call, Mack ran every possible answer through his mind. Nothing made sense. He had never met Siva before and she wasn't someone you forgot. He decided not to wait until tomorrow to find out. After Baxter's call, he'd walk back and pay her a visit.

He glared impatiently at his iPhone willing it to ring.

It worked. The screen came to life and a second later the phone rang. The Caller ID read Sam Baxter.

Baxter, the world's richest man, was not a man to waste time with pleasantries or small talk. He was too busy running Baxter, Israel & Gunn, the world's largest private conglomerate, to engage in small talk. Last year, Baxter personally earned eight billion, seven hundred and sixty-six million dollars, becoming the world's first 'million-dollar-an-hour man.'

"Billy Mack," Baxter said. "I put in three calls to you with no answer. Don't let it happen again."

"I can explain," Mack said.

"You can explain another time. I have Ray Gunn with me. You're closing a key acquisition for us and we haven't heard from you in a week. I trust everything is going smoothly."

"Certainly," Mack replied. He haltingly provided a step-by-step summary of BIG's acquisition of Schwike & Hoffman. S&H was the world's largest provider of corporate security services. He began his report with an incomplete summary of the standard legal issues common in most corporate acquisitions and didn't fully explain each issue. He then gave too much detail when describing the operational differences between the two companies and how he and management had come up with a unique integration plan. His voice had lost its usual assertiveness.

After what happened at the *Prater,* his cadence was labored and he paused a hair longer between sentences. Before Mack could discuss the remaining indemnification issue and give a final summary, Baxter cut him off. "I don't like the sound of your voice or what I heard, Billy Mack. Is there something to worry about with this acquisition?"

"No ..." After a short pause, Mack continued, "So far, no. There is still the sticky issue related to seller indemnification. If it can't be resolved to our satisfaction, I will call you next week to discuss."

"You're not instilling any confidence in me. Is there something going on I should know about?"

Ray Gunn cut in, "Mack, if there is an issue bothering you, we walk away from the deal. Schwike & Hoffman is not the only security firm on the market."

"That's not what's bothering me." Mack took a deep breath and described what happened at *Prater,* leaving out Siva's name and his encounter with the taxi driver on the way back to the hotel.

"Are you certain she said *Jahangir?*" Gunn asked, pronouncing the terrorist group's name like a native Arab.

"Positive," Mack answered. "There was more than a tinge of fear in her voice when she said the name."

The background noise on the phone went silent. Baxter and Gunn had muted their phone. A healthy minute later, the background noise returned.

"Sit tight, Mack," Baxter said. "Ray will make a few calls to some old contacts, see what we can learn."

Ray Gunn was Baxter's business partner. Tall, long and handsome was how women routinely described him. He was a minority owner of BIG and ran the conglomerate's business dealings with governments at home and abroad. Early in his career, Gunn was a Washington DC wiz kid becoming the youngest Secretary of Defense in American history before he opted for the big money corporate world. He was adept at using his Washington contacts to parlay their influence into lucrative defense and intelligence contracts for BIG.

Mack cleared his throat. "I forgot to mention that the woman said my name when I left. She called me William."

Baxter muted the phone again. A half-minute later, he said, "Sit tight, Mack. Don't do anything until we get back to you. It may be a day or so."

"I can work on the S&H indemnification issue while I wait," Mack said. He heard ruffling on the other end of the line and then Gunn's voice vaguely in the distance.

"Hang on," Baxter said and hit the mute button again. A full minute later he came back on the line and asked, "Are you positive this woman called you William?"

"Absolutely, she said *William* clear as day."

"Stay where you are until we have a better handle on the situation and one of us gets back to you."

"I'll be here," he replied knowing it was a lie.

As soon as Baxter hung up the phone, Mack changed into his black jeans, black long-sleeve running shirt and dark gray North Face fleece with a navy blue collar. It was the best he could do.

He strolled through the lobby checking every face. He spotted Karin, the young concierge who had brought him the USB device. She was sitting at her desk writing in a leather bound notebook.

"Karin, I am sorry to have been so busy lately. I hope you understand."

Karin tried not to show her disappointment. "You are here for work, so I understand."

"I will be out of town until Monday, perhaps we can talk when I return."

"I am here all day on Monday."

With the Glock in the pocket of his fleece, he crossed the Ring Road and headed down a side street, keeping in close proximity to groups or couples. With Siva's front door in sight, he stepped into a doorway shadow across the street and check the surroundings for anything suspicious.

Satisfied the area was clear, he strolled to the front door and found Siva's intercom button. It read *Fr. S. Afari, 6 Stock.* Mack pushed and held Siva's intercom button.

No answer.

He pressed the button one more time, then stepped out to the curb and looked up to the sixth floor.

No answer.

He randomly pushed a different call button.

"*Ja, bitte,*" a woman's voice said.

"Hello Siva, it's me," Mack said clearly.

"*Es gibt kein Siva hier,*" the woman said.

Mack pushed another call button.

Five-seconds later, the door lock buzzed open. Mack pushed the door and entered the building's dim entryway. As the door closed behind him he heard a child's voice crackle over the intercom, "*Hallo, Papi.*"

In the musty entryway, a wide, stone staircase wrapped around an old elevator cage. Mack walked into the central courtyard in the back and surveyed the building. There was only one way in or out.

The small elevator consisted of an intricate black metal cage inside a thicker plain black metal cage. Mack gripped the pistol in his pocket, pulled the elevators gates closed behind him and pushed the button for the top floor. At the sixth floor, he crept off the elevator with the Glock in hand. There was only one unit on the entire floor. The apartment's thick, gray metal door had a reinforced brushed metal plate surrounding the door handle. Blood was smeared on the handle and streaked down the metal plate. Blood drops were scattered on the tile floor in front of the door. The blood was sticky. He moved to the side and knocked.

No answer.

Avoiding the blood, he jiggled the door handle. It didn't move. The door was airtight to the heavy metal frame. Without the key, it would take a blast of Semtex or TNT to open this door. He knocked again, harder this time, then stuck his ear against the door. No answer.

On the landing's back wall there was a small window behind the circular stairs and elevator. Its size was closer to a transom than a window. Mack stepped on an overturned metal bucket, pushed open the small window and stuck his head out. An industrial pipe ran up the building between the window and a long, large balcony overlooking the courtyard six stories below. The balcony jutted out leaving a gap of four feet from the building's corner. Below the window, a small ledge ran horizontally along the outside of the building. Mack didn't hesitate. He crawled out the window, grabbed the pipe with both hands and lowered his right foot to the ledge then slowly followed with his left foot. Both his baseball and Taekwondo training were coming in handy. His strong grip allowed him to easily find the right balance. He reached his right hand over and clasped his fingers on the corner of the building. After adjusting his balance, he swung his weight toward the balcony and jumped. His right foot landed on top of the balcony's metal handrail and his momentum propelled his body forward. He landed hard on a round metal table and rolled on to a metal chair, bruising his shin and his forearm. He stifled a profane-laced scream as he limped around the balcony checking his bones. Nothing was broken. Seeing his reflection in the sliding glass door he blocked out the pain. He realized if the balcony door was locked there was no way off the balcony and he would have a lot of explaining to do when Siva returned, if she returned.

He grabbed the handle and pulled. It was unlocked. He waited to see if he triggered an alarm. After forty-five seconds, he exhaled a sigh of relief and stepped inside.

Being a novice at breaking and entering, he wasn't sure if he should turn on the lights. He compromised and used the spotlight app on his iPhone.

Dachwohnungs, or rooftop apartments, were popular in Vienna. *Dachwohnungs* in central Vienna were very exclusive and very expensive, selling for prices between five and fifteen million Euros. From the cavernous size of the room, Mack guessed Siva's apartment fell into the higher end of the price range.

He panned the room with his small spotlight. The apartment's open floor plan had a large, long living area combined with the kitchen and dining space. The room was twenty meters long (62 feet) and ten meters wide (30 feet). The ceiling was four meters high (12 feet).

Persian carpets were spread haphazardly throughout the room. Mack made his way over to a large antique wooden display case centered against the wall. The intricately carved piece of furniture was of Mideast origin. A large framed photograph of Siva and her parents in front of Al Khazneh in Petra, Jordan, was the centerpiece. The resemblance between Siva and her mother was remarkable. Siva and her mother were dressed for the hot desert and looked very happy. Her father was dressed like Indiana Jones without the fedora. Mack shifted the spotlight to the left. He gasped and dropped his phone. Luckily, the phone landed on a plush Persian carpet. He was breathing heavily as he returned the spotlight to the framed photo on the left. It had to be an illusion. He took a hard look this time. It was no illusion.

The soft click of the door lock sounded like a cannon going off. He killed the spotlight on his phone and crept around the corner into the hallway shadows while keeping a clear line of sight to the door.

The door flew open and a glove holding an automatic machine pistol with a suppressor came around the doorjamb.

Mack stepped back further into the shadows.

CHAPTER 6

Sam Baxter built Baxter, Israel & Gunn, commonly called BIG, into the world's largest private conglomerate by identifying trends and anticipating opportunities or problems before they arose. He then acted quickly to capitalize on both. He was nearly six feet tall but due to his frequent television appearances, everyone assumed he was much taller. A two-sport athlete in college, he kept in shape jogging or walking on his office treadmill while talking on the phone.

The call with Billy Mack weighed on his mind. What had Billy Mack gotten himself into? He had sent Mack to Vienna to close a deal, the acquisition of the world's largest security company — everything from renta-cops guarding office buildings, warehouses and shopping malls to sophisticated cyber security. Mack could close the deal with his eyes closed.

BIG's security and defense business was the fastest growing sector in Baxter's empire due to his anticipation in the 1990s of the rapid spread of worldwide terrorism. Using Ray Gunn's government contacts, BIG's defense and security business flourished and was extremely lucrative. The business was also very dangerous. A large segment of the business operated in some of the worst shit holes in the world. Places where despair dominated life and death came as a welcome relief. The more dangerous the situation, the more profitable it was for BIG.

For the last ten years, as the US Government cut defense and intelligence spending more and more operations were outsourced. BIG grew to become the largest independent intelligence contractor to the CIA, the NSA and the DIA.

Baxter had decided it was time to expand BIG's security and defense business into the less dangerous corporate market and reduce the reliance on the US Government. He identified the best companies in the security industry and approached Sunden Capital, an ultra-secretive private equity firm owning a company called Schwike and Hoffman, known in the marketplace simply as S&H.

Baxter's decision to acquire S&H was strategic. S&H, based in Vienna, was the world's largest provider of corporate security services, counting seventy-five percent of the Fortune 1000 companies as clients. Acquiring S&H

was the first step in off-setting BIG's heavy reliance on government contracts. Once the deal was struck, Baxter dispatched Mack to Vienna to close the acquisition.

Based on Mack's last report, the closing of the S&H deal was proceeding as expected. So what was going on in Vienna? Despite ordering Mack to sit tight, Baxter knew he wasn't the type to ride the bench. When he played for the White Sox, Mack was known for manufacturing runs based on his instincts, forcing the opposition to react and usually reacting too late. Baxter asked Rose to go find Ray Gunn.

Baxter poured bourbon over two ice cubes. Looking at Gunn in the mirror behind the bar, he asked, "Why hasn't he checked in?"

The reflection in mirror showed Ray Gunn sitting on the sofa with his feet up, reading. Gunn was a minority owner of BIG, representing the 'G' in the name. "He will," Gunn replied, his mind on autopilot. He wasn't paying attention to Baxter. Gunn lifted the report in his hand and read it again. He read the conclusion a third time and held up the report for Baxter to see.

"This is a copy of the President's Daily Brief from this morning. Every one of the alphabets in the intelligence world as well as the Joint Chiefs are warning the President of an imminent strike against the homeland. It's fucking unanimous. That's never happened before."

"What are our people telling us?" Baxter asked.

"Nothing and I've ordered our signals intelligence team to check sources, see what's up. It bothers me they don't have an inkling of something afoot."

"Has this happened before?"

Gunn grimaced as he shook his head from side to side. "We usually get a head's up."

"Have the team check under every rock. If we're the only ones in the industry out of the loop we have a problem."

Baxter refilled his glass and added two ice cubes. He poured another bourbon, neat this time and walked the glass over to Gunn.

"Thanks," Gunn said and took a sip. "I got a bad feeling. I've been on the phone all day and getting hinky answers to my questions. And, that's only when my questions weren't being artfully dodged."

There was a soft knock on the door and it cracked open. Rose Mueller stepped halfway in and waited for Baxter to wave her in with two fingers.

"I received a call from the *Bundespolizei* in Vienna." Rose annunciated the German word slowly. "That's what the police in Austria are called. You should read the report they emailed," Rose said with tears welling in her eyes. She handed a copy of the report to both men. "It's in English."

Baxter and Gunn read in silence.

"It's him, isn't it? The description fits him." Rose's voice shook. "Why would someone shoot William four times?"

Baxter looked over at Gunn to see if he was going to reply. Neither man knew what to say.

Baxter walked over and hugged Rose. "The description in the report fits but let's not jump to any conclusions. There are two million people in Vienna and

44

a large number of them fit the description."

Baxter knew Rose would be a basket case until there was a confirmation of the victim's identity. "Find someone who speaks German and have them come see me. Then I want you to go home. I will arrange for a call to the *Bundespolizei* to see what we can learn. I will call you when I know more."

Gunn had finished pouring another bourbon by the time the door closed.

"Rose will be devastated," he said softly. "He proposed to her just before he left for Vienna."

Neither man knew what to say. Death was a subject they talked of often and spent very little time considering.

"You asked earlier why he hasn't checked in. Now I think we know why." Gunn downed his entire glass.

Baxter followed suit, downing his glass, and chewing on the ice cubes. "If anyone knew why he was there, we have a Vienna problem."

CHAPTER 7

The size of the hand gripping the silenced machine pistol in the doorway was too big to belong to Siva. The gun slowly pulled back out of sight. Mack gripped the handle of his Glock, keeping his finger above the trigger. He didn't need to accidentally shoot Siva if she was being used as a human shield. In the uneasy silence, Mack went into a crouch and aimed the pistol at the door.

Suddenly, a head darted into the doorway and disappeared just as quickly. The face belonged to the twin he'd knocked out at *Prater* with a kick in the temple. The bruise on his cheek was clearly visible.

The twin leaned his face in, studied the room then

curled his body around the doorjamb with a Steyr Pistol L-A1 in his right hand. A suppressor was attached to the barrel. It wasn't a machine pistol. The gun had been modified to include a longer clip.

Mack moved deeper into the shadows and watched.

Tariq was well trained but impatient as he cleared the apartment. He zigzagged through the living area in complete silence with his pistol in the correct, readied position. He did a cursory trip through the kitchen before heading to the hallway.

Mack had moved down the hall and turned into a dark room before Tariq turned the corner.

Tariq marched past the room heading for a specific destination. Entering the master bedroom, Tariq turned on the light, walked into the master closet, knowing exactly where to go. He bent down and lifted a trap door covering a floor safe. He spun the tumbler, opened the floor safe and took out an envelope. After confirming the contents, he jammed the envelope into his back pocket. Tariq wasn't done. He reached back into the safe, removed three bundles of cash in thousand Euro notes, and shoved two bundles into a pocket inside his biker's jacket.

Walking out counting the third bundle of Euro notes, Tariq let his concentration slip. He strolled past Mack's room with his Steyr pistol in his waistband.

Mack flew out of the doorway aiming his elbow at Tariq's neck. Tariq reacted just in time to deflect Mack's elbow. He turned his head minimizing the blow from Mack and jerked the pistol up from his waistband.

Mack knocked the Steyr from Tariq's hand and kicked it down the hall. Tariq landed a left uppercut into Mack's ribs knocking the air out of him and causing him to drop his Glock. Mack wrapped his arms around Tariq and body slammed him to the floor. Tariq let out a deep grunt, instantly twisted and head-butted Mack in the cheek. Mack lost his grip on Tariq who shot to his feet and stood over him. Sporting an evil grin, Tariq pulled a serrated knife from behind. Before he could swing the knife down, Mack imbedded his right foot into Tariq's testicles. A strange squeal came from somewhere deep inside Tariq. The knife fell from his hand and he dropped to his knees. Mack scrambled out from under, kicked the knife away and gripped Tariq by the nape of the neck, ready to slam his head into the wall. Tariq vomited and passed out.

Mack searched the big man's pockets and took the envelope Tariq had shoved in his back pocket. It contained another USB device; identical to the one Siva slipped him.

In the kitchen, he found twine used for cooking, and bound Tariq's hands and feet. He removed the bundles of cash from Tariq's jacket and returned them to the safe. Removing Tariq's wallet, he found a forged Austrian driver's license and a stolen security ID to the *Prater* amusement park.

Inside Tariq's breast pocket, Mack pulled out a photo. He couldn't believe what he was holding in his hand. He took a more studied look and let the rage build up inside him.

Trying to control his breathing, Mack lost his cool

and unloaded a swift kick into Tariq's ribs. He heard a rib crack. He picked up the Glock and seriously considered using it. He took another long, measured look at the photo. He had to walk away before he did something stupid like shoot the man in cold blood.

The photo showed Mack in sunny Chicago standing outside Navy Pier wearing his blue suit. Next to him was Rose Mueller, Sam Baxter's secretary.

Tariq moaned and moved his head slightly. Mack reached down and snapped his knuckles into Tariq's temple, knocking him back out.

Returning his concentration to the photo, he remembered why he was at Navy Pier. It was a private equity industry conference from earlier in the year. He even remembered when the photo was taken because the person taking the picture was from Sunden Capital and refused to be in the picture or, for that matter, in any picture.

Mack dragged Tariq by the collar of his leather jacket across the apartment, out the door and into the sixth floor landing, closing the door tightly behind him. Whoever went into the apartment next would have to clean up Tariq's calling card.

Still upset, he searched Tariq one final time and found a set of keys. He tested one of the keys in the front door and easily turned the lock. The keys belonged to Siva.

Dragging Tariq's dead weight into the elevator, he kept his right hand ready in case Tariq came to. Able to see through the black cage, Mack breathed a sigh of relief when the building's front entryway was empty. He pocketed Siva's keys and when the elevator hit the ground floor, he hastily pulled Tariq across the entryway to the opposite wall and dumped him behind a blue recycling bin. He cracked the door looking for any Jahangir on the street.

Across the street, a bearded man sat in an idling car trying not to look suspicious. Mack took one final look at Tariq curled up against the stonewall of the entryway, then walked out like a resident heading out to the market. The bearded man in the car was so busy trying to look cool and not attract attention that he didn't see Mack strolling away.

Back inside his hotel suite, Mack stretched out on the sofa. All the signs were there. The blood on Siva's door, the thug from the *Prater* showing up at her apartment and the photo inside the old wooden display case were more than enough to convince Mack she was in trouble.

He closed his eyes. Where was Siva?

CHAPTER 8

Like all five-star hotels, Vienna's Hotel Imperial was known for providing exceptional service with complete discretion. The hotel manager, the concierge and most of the staff proudly repeated this as fact to Mack on a regular basis.

As with everything else in the hospitality industry, money made the rules. Mack rode the elevator to the lobby and approached the front desk. The clerk smiled warmly, like she actually cared. "Do I have any messages?" Mack asked in German.

The clerk typed frantically on the computer then waited. "Yes, Karin, our concierge has put your telephone messages on the desk in your room."

Mack traveled enough to know the staff at five star hotels kept notes about their guests and, more importantly, *detailed* notes on their regular guests and guests staying in the more expensive suites. He slid a hundred Euro note across the counter. "Has anyone inquired about me?"

The clerk returned to the computer and resumed typing. She wrote diligently on a note pad, folded the sheet of paper and slid it across the counter.

Mack casually took the note and noticed the hundred Euro note was gone. He was impressed with her dexterity. On the elevator ride back up to his room, he read the cryptic notes given to him by the desk clerk.

As soon as he locked the door to his room, Mack called Nimesh at his office in Washington DC.

Nimesh, a former Green Beret with a Master's Degree in Computer Science from Carnegie Mellon University, graduated at the top of his class. At five-nine, he had a Buddhist approach to life yet bigger men stepped out of his way when he walked by. In the tech industry, he had the aura of a mystic and was nicknamed "*The Cracker*" by the hacker community. He and his team at *Mira Labs* provided cutting edge cyber security to the largest financial institutions in the world and to the intelligence agencies within the US and UK Governments. The world's best hackers and cyber criminals have only once breached a *Mira Labs* firewall and that was during a testing phase.

Mack skipped the pleasantries when Nimesh answered. "We may have a problem, Nims. A man claiming to be from a company called Wiener Computer

Logistics tried to convince a hotel staffer that he had a work order to service my computer. The staffer described the man as Arabic but spoke fluent German. I was assured no one was granted access to my room."

Mack could hear Nimesh smile. "Welcome to the wonderful world of espionage, Mack. Whoever tried to con their way into your room either wanted the USB device or more likely wanted direct access to your computer. That's the tactic hackers use when they can't breach a computer's firewall remotely."

Mack rotated the USB device he'd taken from Tariq. "I've come into possession of another stick and I bet it's related to the information I showed you yesterday."

"Fire it up."

By the time Mack inserted the USB device in the port, Nimesh had already taken control of Mack's laptop and was performing a security check.

"Someone has been trying to access your computer through the hotel's wifi system. Anytime you use a wireless system, you are vulnerable. The firewalls on your machine are the best but it doesn't stop hackers and crooks from trying. I'm running a tracer to see if I can identify the culprit."

"Do I have anything to worry about?"

"Whenever you use a computer connected to a network, you have something to worry about. I've added a security protocol to your computer so if someone attempts access, I'll receive an alert. Then I'll chase him through cyber space and put a hurtin' on him." Nimesh added, "Or her."

Mack watched his cursor move at light speed while photos and program screens flashed before his eyes. Finally, a listing of program codes appeared and stayed on the screen.

Nimesh asked, "Do you see what's on your screen?" He didn't wait for Mack's answer. "The strings of data are similar to what we looked at yesterday. We have too much data here and it's very sophisticated. We're going to need help and I know just the person. A friend of mine in Switzerland named Susan Baisley is the top cryptologist in the world and one of the leading computer forensic experts. She'll have an algorithm to decode the encryption." The computer screen went black.

"Do you trust her?" Mack asked.

"I trust the Bais with my life."

The computer sprung back to life. Nimesh directed the cursor over the play arrow and the first video filled the screen. The same narrator voice spoke in Persian as a large white Mosque appeared in the center of the screen. Mack didn't need to know Persian to understand what he was seeing. The camera followed a group of soldiers into the white Mosque. The soldiers raised their rifles and ordered the worshipers to get off their knees and line up against the wall.

The General commanding the troops strutted in front of the worshipers, pointing at three men as he went by. A group of soldiers pulled the three worshipers outside. The General resumed strutting in front of the worshipers. He barked an order and the worshipers, including the Imam, turned and faced the wall.

Outside, the three worshipers knelt in the middle

of the dusty, dirty street. The surrounding shops and stalls had pulled down their metal gates or shut their doors. The soldiers had their weapons readied as they stood behind the three kneeling men. The camera panned left to catch the General marching up. Keeping pace on the General's left was the man Mack fought in Siva's apartment. On the right was his identical twin, or was it the other way around. The twin from the General's left sauntered up to the three worshipers kneeling in the hot sun. He slapped the first worshiper across the face and nodded to the General. He slid over to the next worshiper, studied the man and shook his head no. He stepped over to the third worshipper and immediately slapped him hard across the face, nodded again to the General and spoke rapidly in Persian. The narrator on the video repeated what was said.

The worshiper in the middle was kicked in the back by a soldier before he scrambled to his feet, ran up the dusty steps and back into the Mosque. The camera slowly panned back to the street. The General held his pistol against the first worshiper's forehead. He spit in the man's face and pulled the trigger. Blood, tissue and hair splattered on the soldiers standing behind. No soldier dared flinch.

By the time the General had his pistol against the forehead of the third worshiper, the frightened man was talking a mile a minute, fear washing over his face. The General ordered the man to repeat what he'd said. When the worshiper finished his words, the General pulled the trigger. The pistol only clicked. The worshiper wet himself and the General broke into hysterical laughter. He snatched an automatic rifle from one of the soldiers and shot the worshiper six times, five in the chest and as he lay on his back, gave him a final shot in the head.

As the group of soldiers walked away, the narrator, as best Mack could tell, was praying to Allah.

When the video stopped, Nimesh said, "I've taken screen shots of the three men they dragged outside and will run facial recognition through the NSA and CIA data bases. It might take a while."

"Can you include the General and the identical twins?" Mack asked. "The two goons flanking the General are here in Vienna and one of them is in the morgue."

"I'll include them ... How do you know one's dead?"

"It's too complicated to explain now. I'm certain it has to do with what we're watching."

"Do you want to watch the second video?" Nimesh asked with good reason.

"No, but play it anyway."

Mack and Nimesh watched the second video in stunned silence. There was no narration and the location was inside an industrial clean room with no windows. Two long, shiny metal tables were ten feet apart with identical items lying on each. The camera scanned both tabletops.

"That's a nuke bullet," Nimesh said. "There is only one reason to have that."

"Are you certain?"

"Yes, and I see fusion fuel canisters, detonators and Semtex next to three tubes I can't identify. This is all you need to make a small nuke." Nimesh thought about what he'd said. He added, "A small nuke is a misnomer nowadays. Size really doesn't matter when nukes are involved. A bomb this size could still kill millions. Add in a biological and the number doubles."

"We need to light a fire under your friend in Switzerland and figure out what we're—"

Nimesh cut him off. "What's this, down in the right corner on your screen?"

At the bottom-right corner was a tiny symbol of a cross, broken into pieces. Nimesh dragged the cursor over it and right-clicked. A triple password access box popped up over the broken cross.

"Holy shit," Nimesh said. "I need to talk to Susan, see if she's seen this before. What time is it where you are?"

Mack glanced at his watch. "It's coming up on four a.m."

"Susan won't be at her desk for another hour. I can't send her any of this until she gives me an ultra-secure URL."

"What can I do?" Mack anxiously asked.

"Get some rest, you're going to need it."

CHAPTER 9

General Farid impatiently paced through the safe house located on the northern outskirts of Vienna, in the wealthy 19th District. He'd already been outside four times to smoke and check on security. He'd spent six months in this Sodom and Gomorrah of a city and ached to get back to his family compound on the outskirts of his beloved hometown of Qom, in north central Iran.

The General was the director of Iran's top-secret program to fund, arm and direct terrorist groups. Over the years, he developed close personal relationships with every major terrorist group and every sizable splinter group. Six months ago, he was approached personally by the Ayatollah to take a leave of absence from his duties and lead a very special operation out of Vienna, a city he now hated.

He went outside to smoke another cigarette.

Tariq was four hours late. The General began questioning his decision to use the Jahangir for this mission. There was no military discipline with terrorists. They were zealots who think they report only to Allah. Once this operation was over, he would return to only using the Republican Guard.

He couldn't delay the inevitable any longer. Removing the satellite phone from his bag, he punched in the number from memory. It was a call he dreaded making. Not because he feared her, rather he had no respect for her, none.

Unfortunately, Tariq was not back with both devices as the General promised. The failures of the Jahangir were humiliating him.

The General gave the woman a cursory update on the mission and assured he would deliver 'the packages' on time. She cut him off, emphasizing there was no flexibility in the timing of the operation, it was top priority. He fumed at each question she asked, answering as curtly as he could in English, a language he was not comfortable speaking.

As he listened to her rattle on, the front door to the safe house opened and Faruk walked in with Tariq under his arm. Tariq sat down gingerly and Faruk ran to get him some water. A bruised and battered Tariq held his left hand over his ribs.

"I will call you back," the General said into the satellite phone and hung up.

He circled Tariq, studying his bruised cheek and fat lip. If the mission wasn't already short two men, he'd put a bullet between Tariq's eyes for disobeying him. After the mission, the priorities would be different.

"What happened to you?" He asked, knowingly.

"The American agent, this Billy Mack, he attacked me after I finished searching the woman's apartment. He is a CIA trained assassin, I am sure of it."

"I don't care," the General said. "Give me the device you were sent to retrieve."

Tariq looked the General directly in the eye. He said, "It wasn't where she said it would be. She lied to us. There was nothing in the safe but money and documents."

It took every fiber in the General's body for him not to shoot somebody, preferably Tariq.

Faruk came back into the room carrying a glass of water.

"Leave us Faruk," the General ordered.

Faruk placed the glass next to Tariq and hurried away.

The General slapped the glass across the floor. It slid into the far wall and shattered.

"Do not lie to me Tariq. I am much smarter than you and can tell when I am lied to. I will ask you one more time, where is the device?"

Tariq squirmed in his seat keeping direct eye contact. "It was not where she said and I checked the entire apartment. That is where the American assassin attacked me from behind, like a coward."

Gripping Tariq by the chin, the General said,

"Clean up the glass and the water then clean yourself up and wait for your next orders. You are not to do anything, go anywhere or talk to anyone. Do you understand?"

Once Tariq was gone, the General unlocked the door to the cellar and sauntered slowly down the wooden steps. A slow, deliberate pace would surely unnerve her. Instilling the threat of violence in a woman was more effective than hurting her. He would only beat a woman as a last resort.

In the far corner of the dank cellar, Siva sat on a rickety chair with her chin in her chest, asleep. As the General approached, she raised her head slowly. The bruise around her eye, courtesy of Tariq's fist, was beginning to spread. The General cupped her chin, wiped the blood trickling from her nose and lifted her head to examine her eye. Her face would heal without any lasting marks. The deep bruises on her body would take longer to heal. Tariq was especially vicious with the phone book when he beat her.

"You will heal fine," General Farid said in Persian. He was not going to give her the pleasure of speaking English, her native language. "We have a problem. The device we require was not in your safe, as you had said." The General stood behind Siva and leaned into her ear. "I don't want to bring Tariq back down. He enjoys killing too much and I may accidentally let him have his wish."

"Your Tariq is lying to you," Siva said. "Inside my safe was thirty-thousand Euros, my travel documents and the USB stick in a sealed envelope, nothing else."

General Farid had risen quickly through the

Republican Guard and one of the reasons for his quick assent was his ability to read people. Women, to the contrary, were extremely difficult for him to read. It required constraint, coercion and control, just the right amount of control.

"Why was the American at your apartment? You lied about your relationship with him."

Siva didn't hide her surprise. "There was no one in my apartment when your men dragged me out. Both your thugs searched the apartment." There was no fear in her voice.

"How did he get inside?"

Siva relaxed slightly. "How do I know?" Siva had to buy time. "I can ask him when I see him this afternoon. We are scheduled to meet again at the *Prater*."

The General studied Siva's beautiful face. If he weren't consumed by his mission, he would take her upstairs to his quarters right now and let her perform her womanly duties. "I should take you to my bed to see if you are better than Zoya. Unfortunately I will have to wait for that pleasure until after my mission."

Siva spat on the ground. "Never."

He slapped Siva hard across the cheek. "I do not tolerate disrespect. When I am finished, you will serve every desire I demand."

Siva squeezed her lips tightly together and held in her rage.

"I will let you go. You will meet with this Billy Mack as if nothing happened and get the devices back from him. If you try anything, my people will kill you both."

Siva pointed to her cheek and nose.

"Before you meet him, I will have someone take you back to your apartment so you can cover your bruises."

Standing from the chair, every muscle in Siva's body screamed in pain.

The General shoved her back into her seat. "Before you go, tell me who gave you the computer sticks."

"I already told you, they were sent separately by courier. The return address didn't exist."

General Farid yelled for a Jahangir named Hamid to come downstairs and ordered him to take Siva back to her apartment.

Hamid gently placed a hood over Siva's head and helped her up the stairs.

"Remember Siva, if you do something stupid it will be the last thing you do," the General yelled.

Upstairs, General Farid laughed as he watched Faruk scrubbing the wall and floor with cleaning compounds he had found in the kitchen. Faruk struggled to scrub the blood completely out of the grout between the tiles and finally gave up when he jammed his thumb.

He backhanded the cleaning bucket and sent it flying into General Farid's legs. His laughter stopped.

"You are lucky, Faruk that nothing was spilled on my uniform pants. You can stop cleaning. We are going to burn the house when we leave."

Faruk remained on his knees, cowering as the General kicked the bucket back over to him.

"Where is Tariq?"

Faruk pointed at the back porch. "He is smoking."

"I wish to speak with him," the General said. When Faruk didn't move, the General grabbed him by the scruff of the neck and shoved him toward the porch doors. "Tell him I want to see him in the mission room now, not in two minutes, not in one minute, now." The General marched out of the room and up the steps.

Thirty-seconds later, Faruk stood in the doorway of the mission room ready to bolt the other way as soon as the General reached for his sidearm. He stroked his thick black beard and stuttered as he began to speak.

"Ta ... Tar ... Tariq is not in the back smoking anymore. I cannot find him."

CHAPTER 10

Mack was basically a night person. Most professional baseball players and former players were night people. Games were mainly played in the evenings, ending between nine and ten. After the game, players liked to unwind. During his playing days, it was usually after two a.m. before Mack turned in for the night.

William McMillan signed his first professional baseball contract the day he graduated from high school. Playing baseball, he was known simply as Billy Mack. He spent his first three years enduring the all night bus trips to the next minor league town before he caught a break and became the starting third baseman for the Chicago White Sox. When he reached *The Show*, it was good-bye to the all-night buses ... and hello to all-night plane flights. Mack never complained. He was getting paid to play a game. On his thirty-fourth birthday, his career ended long before he was ready. In the very last game of his thirteenth season, he broke his right arm and dislocated the elbow and shoulder in a violent collision at home plate. It wasn't the birthday present he expected. After an offseason of rehab, he was still unable to throw a baseball more than fifty feet and had to walk away from the game.

The owner of the White Sox, Sam Baxter, offered Mack a courtesy job at BIG glad-handing clients, attending corporate functions and motivating employees. When Baxter realized Mack had the chops for business, he began assigning him tough assignments like corporate acquisitions or the dirty work of fixing failing companies and divisions. Mack, eager for a challenge, rolled up his sleeves and thrived.

Lying awake in the large bed, the image of the Mosque worshipers kneeling on the dusty street and getting their brains blown out replayed in Mack's head as he tried to sleep. Every half hour he would climb out of bed and gaze out the window at the dark city before crawling back into bed.

At seven-fifteen, Mack was gazing out the hotel window, his mind reconstructing the fight in Siva's apartment trying to figure out how he let the intruder get the better of him.

Low gray clouds hovered over the city and the people on the streets below carried unopened umbrellas. He looked over the tops of the buildings trying to determine which rooftop belonged to Siva. That's when a thought nagged at him. How did Siva afford a *Dachwohnung*? Unless she inherited a fortune or married money, she had to earn a pretty penny to afford such a place. Mack didn't recall seeing any evidence of a husband in the apartment so Siva had to get the money elsewhere. What did she do to afford a multi-million dollar apartment?

A soft knock on his door surprised him. He threw on a pair of jeans and checked the door camera. On the small black and white screen was Karin, the concierge, dressed in her street clothes, a tight, and revealing double layer tank top and form-fitting blue jeans. If she was carrying a weapon, it was well concealed. She smiled sweetly up into the camera.

Why was she knocking on his door this early in the morning? He ran a variety of scenarios through his mind.

When Mack opened the door, Karin walked into the room just far enough to allow Mack to close the door. She lifted her hand and handed him a folded sheet of paper.

"When I arrived at my desk this morning, this note was there."

Mack dug into his pocket for his money.

Karin held up her hand. "No, I cannot accept your money." She deliberated as she turned and twisted nervously. "I couldn't wait until Monday," she said shyly. "When we had our dinner, I said I would go to practice my English. As we talked I realized I enjoyed your company." She blushed. "I liked talking with you and I would like to have a lunch or dinner with you again." She dropped her eyes as if she feared his answer.

He said, "I tell you what. I am busy for the next couple nights. If my schedule does not change, we can have dinner on Tuesday. If that is fine with you."

She beamed. "Thank you, yes, that would be very fine. If you wish, I know a traditional Austrian restaurant and we can meet us there. I will make the reservation and leave a note for you at the front desk with the address and directions."

"I look forward to it." Mack went to his briefcase for his wallet. "I have a request for you. Can you pick something up for me?"

"Of course."

Mack gave her two hundred Euros. "I need a cheap cell phone, the cheapest you can buy with the smallest pay-as-you-go amount."

Karin pocketed the money. "I will leave the mobile phone at the front desk for you." She turned to go, paused, then spun back around. "Until we see us on Tuesday."

As he closed the door, Mack watched the young blonde bounce down the hall to the elevators.

It felt good to have his self-esteem bolstered. As a reward, he punched the room service button on the phone and ordered a traditional Austrian breakfast of meats and cheeses with orange juice and coffee. He splashed some water on his face and was patting his chin dry when the hotel phone rang. Probably room service calling back.

"Servus, my friend. Did I wake you?"

Mack instantly recognized the voice. "Servus, Rainer. You didn't wake me, I had to get up to answer the phone."

"You need a new comeback, Billy," Rainer replied with a laugh. "You've been using that line since we were in high school."

"And you've been laughing at it since high school."

"We will see you this evening, right?"

"You may not want to after I tell you what's happened." Mack gave Rainer a less than detailed account of events at the *Prater*, the fight in Siva's apartment and his plans to return to the *Prater*. "I don't know how safe it is for you, Bettina and the kids."

There was a soft confidence in Rainer's voice. He said, "We are not going to let you get off so easily. Remember, the train departs Hauptbahnhof at six and I will pick you up at the Bahnhof in Bad Vöslau at six thirty."

"Can't wait. I will see you at six thirty."

Mack showered hoping the hot water would invigorate his tired, sore body. He shaved and before he finished dressing, room service knocked on his door. He nearly opened the door before he took a glance at the video screen.

Mack didn't like what he was seeing in the hallway. On the small screen an Arab in a hotel uniform fidgeted as he stood behind the food service cart. His head remained bowed and slightly turned away from the camera as if he were afraid to be recognized.

Mack hurried to the bedroom and yelled, "I will be right there." He tossed on a hotel robe and pocketed the Glock. The pistol was too heavy and pulled down on the robe. He abandoned that idea, pulled on a pair of pants, jamming the pistol in the waistband and loosely tied the robe, covering only half the pistol.

The room service attendant pushed the cart across the room to the seating area with his eyes glued to the butt of the pistol in Mack's waistband. He removed the metal plate covers and poured the coffee. His nametag said *Samir*. He handed Mack the bill. Mack was not about to take his eyes off the Samir's hands and accidentally signed the bill in the middle, nowhere near the signature line. He handed Samir a ten Euro note and opened the door. Samir's brown eyes were hollow as he crumpled the ten Euro note into a ball and tossed it on the floor.

In a low voice, he said, "Bring both devices to Prater when you go or your girlfriend dies." He unfolded and held up sheet of paper with a grainy photo of Siva bruised and bleeding from the nose.

On the small black and white security screen Mack watched Samir walk away, remove his room service jacket and drop it in front of the elevators.

Mack prepared his food then couldn't muster the courage to eat. He sniffed each item wondering if he knew what poison smelled like or if you could even smell poison. He turned on his computer and searched the Internet for information on detecting poisons in food. He was letting his paranoia run amok. He reached to power down the computer.

Before he touched the power button, his screen went black and Nimesh appeared on half the screen. On the other half, a woman with her light brown hair pulled back into a ponytail and wearing black cat eyeglasses appeared. Nimesh introduced Susan Baisley.

"Susan works in Switzerland, and Mack, that is all you need to know. The Bais and I have been trying to decipher the second USB. The level of security is as sophisticated as there is. Whoever enciphered this device had access to systems not available outside of government agencies. Luckily, the Bais is the best cryptologist and computer forensics expert in the world."

Susan was used to her wearing her veil of secrecy without explanation and delved right in. It avoided having to explain why she couldn't explain. "Where did you get this device?"

Mack gave her a quick and dirty summary of the incidents at the *Prater* and Siva's apartment.

"Did the twin brother you encountered at the apartment have a scar on his chin in the shape of a v?"

"No, he had no visible scars."

"Then the man you killed at the *Prater* was Taher Zarif. He was number two in the Jahangir and running the day to day operations. His twin brother, the man you knocked out at the *Prater* and the apartment is Tariq Zarif. He is the Jahangir's top assassin. When Iran orders the Jahangir to kill a high-ranking government official or a high value target anywhere in the world, Tariq is sent. In Tariq's file at the CIA there are twenty-seven confirmed kills attributed to him. According to his profile, he is determined, dangerous and deranged."

"Tread carefully, Mack," Nimesh said. "You killed his brother and he will hunt you to the ends of the earth to exact his revenge. The only way to stop him is to kill him."

"It's worse than that," Susan added. "You killed his *twin* brother."

"What a great way to start my day."

"If you want some good news, Tariq is like a bull in a china shop," Susan said.

"How is that good news?"

"You will definitely see him coming."

Susan put the picture of a smiling General on the screen. "The commanding officer in the video is General Hafez Farid of the Republican Guard. Until six months ago, he headed Iran's secret program to fund and arm terror groups around the world. Sources inside Iran say at one time he was heavily involved in the development of Iran's nuclear program. There has been no confirmed sighting of him inside Iran for the past six months. For him to surface in Vienna has the CIA and Mossad falling over each other. I've never seen them this worried."

"He's a sick bastard," Nimesh said. "I saw the results of his handiwork during my last two tours in Iraq."

"What the hell's he doing in Vienna?" Mack asked.

Susan said, "I've put out some feelers and I'm getting the cold shoulder. That's a very bad sign."

The picture of the General holding his pistol on the forehead of the worshiper kneeling in the street emerged on the screen.

"The man he shot in cold blood was a Palestinian.

He was an agent being run by the Mossad. This was confirmed to me unofficially. The Mossad is working on various plans to destroy Iran's nuclear program from within and Iran has been relentless at ferreting out traitors or agents. All it takes is one allegation, true or not and there is no trial."

A still photo of the third worshipper with five holes in his torso and one in his head came on the screen. "The man shot six times was Kurdish and I am still working on why he was in Iran. The Mossad has nothing on him. The Kurds and the Iranians hate each other so I am surprised to find a Kurd, even an Iranian Kurd working for the Iranians."

The screen went black and computer code scrolled up filling the screen.

Nimesh said, "The Bais and I have been analyzing the string of embedded code from the first device and have deciphered some of it. It looks to be instructions, directions and contact information. The first chunk we've highlighted on the screen is the location of a specially equipped van. The location is a local rental center on the other side of the Hungarian border. The van has already been picked up. Austria does not have any street cams in the area so we are shit out of luck trying to identify where the van crossed the border. There is an APB out for the van but you can bet it's been repainted and carries stolen plates."

Susan Baisley said, "The second chunk of code we've highlighted instructs the intended recipients where and when to obtain forged travel documents. I made a call to a contact in the Austrian security services and gave him this information. It was old news. A few days ago the country's top Cobra team, they are Austria's special ops squads, was called into a grizzly situation by neighbors complaining about the smell coming from the old building. It turns out to be the same location indicated in the code. They found the body of Austria's top forger. His head had been separated from his body. Evidence was found indicating he altered valid passports of ten Austrians. All ten passport holders died mysteriously and during the same week, only days before the dates indicated in the code. The names have been added to Interpol's database. There's a big caveat here. The forger was considered the Picasso of Austrian forgers. You can bet he changed the names to be Arabic or Persian and altered the passport data."

"So basically we have a van we can't find and ten altered passports we can't identify," Mack said.

Susan said, "Patience, Mr. McMillan. We are still piecing together the puzzle. You didn't think these terror jockeys were going to make it easy for us, did you?"

"The Bais won't let you down, Mack."

"Were you able to open the broken cross icon?"

Susan said, "We are still working on it. We are making progress. The first password opened a link to the website of a company called Schwike & Hoffman. It is some kind of hacking instruction but when we attempted, we were shut down. Don't worry Mr. McMillan, we haven't run across a site we can't enter or a code we can't break."

"Did you say Schwike & Hoffman?"

"Yes, it's a company based in Vienna."

"I know the company well, BIG is buying it. Are you sure it's Schwike & Hoffman?"

"Yes, but it appears to be a link to a subsidiary called Sterling Silver. We need more time to analyze the links."

"That's a problem. I have to bring both devices to the *Prater* in a few hours. General Farid has taken Siva and is threatening to kill her if I don't deliver the devices. I'm out of options."

"Maybe you aren't." Susan said. "I can add a cutting edge encryption to the first device but not the second ... yet. Once I embed the encryption, here's what you do."

CHAPTER 11

At the last minute, Sam Baxter changed his plans and accompanied Ray Gunn on the corporate jet to Washington DC. Gunn's trip was a fact-finding mission. He was meeting with BIG's liaison with intelligence agencies and high-level contacts within the CIA. What Gunn wanted to learn could only be accomplished face to face. He didn't trust any other form of communication. Baxter came along because he also had a number of unanswered questions.

Earlier in the day, Gunn confirmed the dead body in the Vienna morgue was William Walters; a former DIA agent who handled special projects for BIG. Walters, a former Defense Department prodigy of Gunn, had been sent by Gunn to assist the CIA in its investigation of a security breach within the IAEA, the International Atomic Energy Agency headquartered at the UN in Vienna. Inside the UN, the IAEA was referred to as "The Agency."

Only one person, Casey Ryan, the CIA Station Chief in Vienna, knew Walters' identity and presence in Vienna. William Walters, a highly regarded former operative, was too experienced to blow his cover. Somebody learned of Walters' presence in Vienna.

Gunn knew Casey Ryan well and was confident he was not the leak. In a tense phone conversation, Ryan assured Gunn that Walters' death would be avenged and no record of his visit to Vienna would be recorded by any Austrian government agency. His body was already on a diplomatic plane en route to Washington. The CIA team stationed in Vienna would lead the investigation of Walters' murder. Once the perpetrator or perpetrators were found, they would quietly disappear.

A larger concern by Ryan was the whereabouts of Siva Afari, a CIA source inside the Agency. He had tried to contact her through his usual channels, getting no answer. His concern was heightened based on recent IAEA reports made privy to him by Siva.

On multiple occasions, Siva expressed concerns about a breach of protocol within the Agency. Evidence came to light inside the IAEA of altered reports on Iran's nuclear program making it look like Iran was scaling back its enrichment program. As required in the recent agreement between Iran and the Agency, these falsified reports were being sent to the United States as valid.

None of the Iranians working at the Agency knew Siva spoke Persian and spoke freely around her. They were under the impression she was a Sunni Arab and secretly detested her.

When Siva's investigation uncovered the altered reports, the CIA resurrected its sleeper agent inside Iran's Republican Guard to investigate. The agent inside Iran would provide detailed intelligence through Siva in her role at the IAEA. When the White House got wind of the plan, they delayed the implementation, effectively killing the operation.

Last month, Siva stopped receiving her communications from Iran. Then four days ago, the first USB device arrived via courier with instructions to hand it off directly to an operative at a pre-arranged location and time. She was given detailed instructions for the drop at *Prater* and a description of Walters.

Casey Ryan had called BIG and personally requested Walters as the liaison for the operation. He'd used Walters on other covert missions. After increasing the fee paid to BIG, Baxter and Gunn immediately agreed and Walters was dispatched to Vienna.

Gunn reached across the aisle and tapped Baxter on the arm. "What do we do about Mack?" His words were barely audible over the hum of the jet engines.

It was not a question Baxter was prepared to answer. "With Walters gone, we have nobody in Vienna. Mack is more than capable if given guidance but he's not trained."

Ray Gunn's approach to business was more military than MBA. Have a plan and detailed strategy then take what you could get and if there was a problem sort it out later.

"Until we know what happened to Walters, we may want to slow down the S&H deal," Gunn said. "S&H is the contract security firm for the UN and specifically for the IAEA."

Baxter nearly fell over. Ray Gunn was pulling in the reins. "What the hell have you done with Ray Gunn?"

Gunn remained serious. He had something on his mind. "The more I'm learning, the more I suspect something nefarious is afoot," Gunn replied. "The whole Iranian connection inside the UN is unnerving. If there is an international incident, you can bet the UN's contract security agency will take the fall. If we buy S&H and the shit hits the fan at the UN, we just bought a bunch of empty uniforms. I guess what I'm saying is we either extricate Mack or get him some personal protection. In either case, we proceed with caution on the acquisition."

Baxter deliberated. "How long will it take to get him protection?"

"At least forty-eight hours ... probably more."

"Make the call. In the meantime, I will tell Mack to slow walk the acquisition. Let me use your phone, mine is in my bag."

"It's the middle of the night there. Let's wait and see what we learn from the alphabets in DC before we talk to Mack."

Gunn realized he forgot to shave. On the way to the sink in the plane's sleeping quarters, he asked, "Who's going to break the news of Walters' death to Rose?"

CHAPTER 12

"Okay newbie, this should get you started," Susan Baisley said as she logged off. Lucky for Mack her instructions were easy to follow. Feeling like a neophyte hacker, he cracked his knuckles and began typing. He was not a computer geek by any stretch of the imagination but was proficient with the software programs used for his work and could surf the net as well as anybody. Not being a heavy user of the popular social and networking sites, he liked to say he was *old school*, preferring direct contact. If he wanted to find out what someone was up to, he picked up the phone or made arrangements to meet up.

He printed out the screen shot of the strings of embedded code, opened the S&H website and familiarized himself with every page of the site. He read every word, clicked on every link and icon looking for a match to the letters, numbers and symbols in the string of code. Clicking over to the Sterling Silver site, he found nothing out of the ordinary. Sterling Silver was an aviation company. After an hour he gave up, hoping Nimesh or Susan would have some luck.

It wasn't a complete waste of time. He'd learned more about S&H, the company whose acquisition he was leading. S&H was a market leader in nearly every one of its divisions. The airport security division guarded every major airport in Europe and most regional airports. They owned S&H Jet Leasing, the world's largest private jet leasing company and just signed a billion dollar contract with the American government to provide sky marshals for every international flight to and from America. The more he'd read about S&H, the more he realized Baxter was buying a strong company at a great price.

He had two hours before his second meeting with Siva ... if she shows up. He uploaded a map of *Prater* and memorized the layout for points of access and potential escape routes. He planned to arrive thirty minutes early and scout the area before he took the same seat at the beer garden.

As the rendezvous time neared, he locked his computer and passport inside the room's safe and stuck the Glock into the waistband at the small of his back. He rode down the elevator with a well-dressed Italian couple. For the entire ride down, the couple talked over each other. When the door dinged open, they both stopped talking and smiled lovingly at each other as they exited

arm in arm. Mack followed them out and headed toward
the concierge desk.

Mack couldn't believe his eyes. He jumped into
the hallway leading to the guest restrooms and peeked
around the corner.

Tariq stood at the concierge desk with his hands
on each corner, leaning in close. He had a big smile on his
face as Karin typed on her computer keyboard. Karin
finished typing and said a few words as she nodded her
head. Tariq's smile disappeared. He shook his finger at
her, spun around and marched out the door.

Mack entered the men's room, splashed water on
his face and took his time drying his face and hands.
When he strode into the lobby, Karin was no longer at
her desk.

Mack pulled out the card in his pocket and called
the number at the bottom.

By the time Mack pushed through the revolving
door the taxi was in front waiting.

"Mr. John Wayne, you finally call."

Mack tried to think of a reason not to get into the
taxi. The best he could come up with was the driver was a
smart ass. The tug at his gut prevailed upon him to crawl
into the back seat and close the door.

Gotta do whatcha gotta do.

Mack realized the taxi was a different car than
from before. He was sitting in the backseat of a Mercedes
E300.

"You are driving a new car today, Mr. ... by the
way what is your name?"

"You can call me Shah, like Shah of Iran."

In the rearview mirror Mack saw Shah wink at him like it was an inside joke.

"Like the Shah of Iran, uh? Are you Iranian?"

"No, I like sound of Shah. I am from Soran clan in Kurdistan."

Shah continued, "I am very happy to having you call. Before you calling, I drive customer who very much important at the United Nations. When customer have meeting in Vienna, I always called. I am trusting, know what I am meaning."

"Why doesn't the UN provide him a car?" Mack asked just to make conversation. He was more concerned with making his approach through the *Prater* and to the beer garden without being seen.

"My customer knowing I am trusting."

Mack wasn't paying attention. He had bigger things on his mind. Seeing a little used entrance to the *Prater*, he said, "Pull over here." He handed forty Euros to Shah.

"I no take money. This is trip for my apologies."

"Thank you. Wait near the front entrance. If anything changes, I will call and let you know where to meet."

Shah nodded. "You call and trusting I be on time. Please to remember this." Shah leaned his head out the window. "I am waiting in front and to you for calling."

Mack jogged across the street and entered the *Prater*. Recalling the map he'd memorized, he made concentric circles through the amusement park as he approached the beer garden, keeping his eyes open for anything unusual. Exactly what, he didn't know. He tried to visualize what a typical terrorist looked like. He didn't have an answer but in his mind all terrorists resembled Tariq Zarif.

Ten minutes before Siva was expected to arrive, he sat at the same table. The beer garden was much less crowded. He ordered a beer, practicing his German on the waitress. She answered him in English.

By the time the waitress left with his order, the tables on each side of him were occupied by two rough, dark-skinned, bearded men resembling Tariq. The two men were not subtle, smiling dangerously as they tapped their jackets on left side of their chest, where a shoulder holster would be found.

Exactly ten minutes later, Siva strolled past the ice cream stand without stopping and weaved cooly through the tables in the beer garden. She wore a colorful headscarf and a large pair of black Gucci sunglasses. Her face was nearly covered. There was a confidence in her stride accompanied by an air of righteousness. Arriving at Mack's table, she spoke in Persian to the two men sitting on each side of Mack, ordering them to move away. They moved to tables out of earshot.

She removed her headscarf and sunglasses, let her hair fall over the side to hide the bruises on her face and greeted Mack with a kiss on each cheek.

"What happened to your eye?" he asked.

"It will heal." She pushed her hair gently back in order to see better. "I am sorry for the situation we find ourselves in. I made a terrible mistake when I mistook you for William Walters. I was so nervous I did not give you a chance to speak. This is my fault."

"It doesn't matter. I've done my homework and we have bigger problems to deal with at the moment."

"That is true. We have a bad situation and it is only going to get worse," Siva said. "If we don't give them what they want, they will kill us both."

Mack was not about to accept Siva's *fait accompli*. It may be the bottom of the ninth but he still had an at-bat coming up.

"With apologies to Yogi Berra, every baseball player knows it ain't over 'til it's over."

Siva looked at him strangely.

Mack said, "If we give them what they want, they will kill us both."

Siva slumped in her seat. "I am sorry I did not have time to warn you. I had no choice but to come here today."

"Sit up," Mack said. "Act like we are in control, like we are the ones in charge."

Siva couldn't believe her ears. "What is it with you Americans?" she said, sitting up straight.

"Hear me out. This is what we're going to do. We give them what they want and we don't give them what they want."

Siva rolled her eyes. "That doesn't make sense."

"What ever happens, when Tariq arrives, I do the talking. You follow my lead."

A thick dark cloud covered the sun and a cold wind blew into the park. As if on cue, everything inside the *Prater* came to a grinding halt. Siva clenched Mack's hand.

General Farid marched down the main *Prater*

walkway as parents cleared their children from his path. He was Moses parting the sea, Sherman burning the South. He never took his eyes off Mack.

"What is he doing here?" Mack said, trying to read Siva's face.

"I had no choice."

"No, I expected Tariq, the man who attacked you, not General Farid."

"You know General Farid?"

"I do my homework."

The General sat across the round table from Mack, whistled at the waitress and waved her over. She turned and walked the other way.

"That is what is wrong with your women," General Farid said, pointing at Mack. "They do not know their place."

"That's a true statement if you consider women property."

"They have their usefulness, if they keep their place."

"Does your wife agree with you?" Mack asked.

"Yes, all of them. I have three wives — one for the kitchen, one for the cleaning and one for the bedroom. They each know their place."

"You're a lucky man."

The General understood sarcasm. With a proud smile, he changed the subject. "Do you have what belongs to me?"

Mack opened the palm of his left hand. "You're referring to this, I presume."

"There is only one device," General Farid said as

he reached for the USB device. Mack pulled his hand back. "Not so fast, General. We need to come to an agreement before you get anything."

"I agree. Here are my terms. If you don't give both devices to me, I will kill you where you sit and take the spoils of war that are left." With a wicked smile, he winked at Siva. "That is, until she no longer satisfies me."

"If I hand you both devices, you'll kill both of us."

General Farid's laugh was sharp and short. "I have promised Tariq the pleasure of killing you. I have not decided what I do with Siva Afari when we leave here. It would be a pity to kill such beauty."

Mack needed to buy time until Siva was released and out of danger. "As I agreed, you will get both USB devices but there is a catch. Experts have encrypted this device. Even if you have the best algorithms in the world, it will still take a year to decipher the encryption. Do you want to take that chance?"

The General wiggled the large handgun on his lap, no longer hidden underneath the table.

Mack had to give the General his due. He was very good at intimidation. Showing fear would only feed his hostility. "There is one other thing, General. If you attempt to decipher the encryption and input the wrong code, the USB sticks are wiped clean and the data is unrecoverable."

The General slipped the handgun back into his shoulder holster. "What are your terms?"

"After Siva walks away, I hand you this device. Then I walk away. In one hour I will call you with the password for the device. It's marked with an A. Once I am certain Siva and I are safe, I will call you with instructions for the exchange of the second stick, marked B."

General Farid stared at Siva. "You may leave."

Every muscle in Siva's body ached as she stood. She would not give the General the satisfaction of seeing her suffer. Her glare matched the hate he was casting at her. She gave away no other emotion, put on her sunglasses and cooly strolled out of the beer garden.

When she turned the corner in the direction of the main entrance, Mack handed the USB device to General Farid.

"If I do not get the password and the other device as we agreed Mr. Mack, I will find you both and kill you — slowly."

"I assume you are planning to do that anyway."

The General's sharp laughter turned heads across the beer garden. "No, as I said, I leave that for Tariq. He must revenge the murder of his brother. Tariq will not rest until he has honored his brother with your painful death."

"This is the part where I leave." Mack placed a cheap flip phone on the table. "I will call you on this phone for our next rendezvous."

"One more thing, Billy Mack, that is what you are called as a famous baseball player, no? I always think one step ahead of my enemies."

General Farid held up his phone showing Mack a picture. "If you do not give me the code and device as agreed, your girlfriend will be shot and dumped on street in front of your lawyer's office."

Mack's body twitched. How the hell did he know about her?

General Farid's eyes darkened. "I know as much about you as I suspect you know about me. There is one thing you must remember, I always win."

Strolling away, Mack didn't look back and caught up to Siva at the main entrance. Shah flashed the taxi's lights to get Mack's attention. He and Siva hurried into the Mercedes.

Shah ignored Mack. "A thousand apologies for what I said last time we meet," he said to Siva in Persian.

"We must leave right now," Siva said urgently. She shook the driver's seat from behind. "We have a big problem running after us."

Fifty meters behind, Tariq was sprinting through the main plaza with his black Steyr pistol in his hand.

The tires squealed as Shah curled around traffic, turned left through a red light, barely missed colliding with a delivery truck and drove down the street. Out the back window, Tariq kept running. He was in a full sprint and gaining on the taxi. He fired his pistol, missing high. Shah hit the gas pedal and ran the next three red lights as Tariq faded from sight.

"To where do you want me to driving?" Shah asked.

"*Hauptbahnhof*, we have a train to catch at six o'clock."

Shah glanced at his watch. "I hope you are making."

CHAPTER 13

The landing at Washington Dulles International Airport was hard and quick due to the strong, gusty winds. Right after the wheels touched down the pilot braked so hard Baxter and Gunn were slammed back into their seats. The plane seemed to pull a muscle and limped off the runway to the Silver Sterling terminal. Silver Sterling was the Fixed Base Operator owned by Schwike & Hoffman, the company BIG was about to acquire.

The Limousine was parked in the usual spot on the tarmac with the back door open. Baxter always sat in the back seat of a limo and faced forward. Gunn preferred the side seat facing the driver's side.

Exiting the airport, both men checked their

phones for any emails, voice mails and text messages. Baxter's phone rang while he was reading his emails.

"Baxter," he said, then listened for five minutes. There was no opportunity to interrupt or even acknowledge being on the other end of the line.

Gunn strained to listen to the tinny voice coming out of Baxter's phone.

Baxter finally spoke, "I will see what I can do but can't promise anything until I get a trained agent in Vienna."

"Was that who I think it was?" Gunn asked.

"Yes, and I don't understand why he called me and not you."

"Because Ryan used to work for me before he joined the CIA and if there's a problem, he's probably embarrassed. What did he say?"

"He had an agent with a loose trail on Mack, nothing official. Our boy has been busy. He's also very good. Who would have thought Mack could elude the CIA."

"What has he been up to?" Gunn asked.

"He went back to the drop zone and met Siva Afari again. This time they were surrounded by bad guys. Somehow, Mack and Siva were able to walk away while the Iranians sat and watched."

"How the hell did he pull that off?"

Baxter had seen Mack make extraordinary plays on the baseball field, plays no normal human could possibly make. He played with an intuition and an anticipation you couldn't teach. "He may be as good an agent as he was a ballplayer."

Coming into downtown Washington, Baxter ordered the limo driver to pull over across from a small park on D Street and made the call.

"We're at Spirit of Justice Park," he said. After a short pause, he answered, "On our way."

Gunn gave the directions to the driver.

"Are you sure?" the driver asked. "I know the street well."

"I'm certain. I used to live there."

Following the directions, the limo driver turned onto New Jersey Avenue, turned again on the first side street and found the long thin driveway. The limo barely squeezed between the buildings. As he approached the graffiti-filled wall in front of him, the wall lowered.

"Way cool! Just like the freakin' Batcave," the driver said.

"Stay in the car," Gunn ordered as he and Baxter exited.

A young black woman stood in the dimly lit doorway. Her face lit up as Gunn approached.

"Uncle Ray," she said as she hugged him. "My dad is in his study. He's been talking about you coming to visit all day."

"It's great to see you, Donna. You look as lovely as ever." Gunn introduced her to Baxter and she led them into the house, down a short hallway to a study with its walls lined with books.

Dave Bridges sat in his electric wheelchair nervously tapping his pen on his desk.

"I see you have some new wheels," Gunn joked.

"The Mercedes of chairs. The only thing it can't

do is climb stairs ... yet." Bridges drove his chair around his desk.

Gunn leaned down and hugged him tightly. "Dave, this is my partner Sam Baxter."

"The richest man in America. It's an honor, Mr. Baxter."

Baxter stuck out his hand. "It's Sam and the honor is all mine."

Baxter remembered Bridges' story well. It was the lead story on the evening news for a week. The President was in Iraq on a surprise visit to the troops and an Iraqi insurgent dressed as a soldier was mistakenly allowed to enter the hanger where the President was about to address the troops. As the President strolled to the podium, the Iraqi charged with a pistol in his hand. Bridges, the DIA's most prolific agent in Iraqi Kurdistan, reacted first, wrestled the Iraqi to the ground and took a round in the neck and two rounds in the abdomen. He snapped the attacker's neck but nearly bled to death in the process. The gunshots paralyzed him from the waist down.

Gunn knew Bridges from his days at the DIA and after he recovered, hired him to handle BIG's relationship with the intelligence agencies and to consult on security matters.

"You boys better settle in for the story I'm about to tell you." Bridges wheeled over and poured three single malt scotches. "First, we need a little thinking man's elixir." He handed the half-filled tumblers to Gunn and Baxter.

He parked his chair behind his desk and pushed a

button on his desktop. Steel shades rolled down covering the windows, the lights enhanced to softly light the room and a muted drone emanated from the ceiling.

"No one can hear us now," he said.

Baxter studied the books lining the walls, staying out of hearing distance and letting Gunn and Bridges briefly catch up on family. The book collection lining the walls was diverse with a heavy emphasis on Mideast history.

"Sam, come and join us," Bridges said.

Baxter settled in the leather chair next to Gunn.

Bridges aimed the remote control at the wall and a flat screen dropped from the ceiling. After a couple of taps on his keyboard, a picture of General Farid in his uniform came on the screen. Behind him was a large white Mosque.

"We all know this psychopath. He's been in Vienna for the past few months. During that time, a team of ten from the Jahangir has joined him. They've secured a safe house and have done a masterful job keeping the location secret. In my last communication with Walters, he had a lead on the location. I believe he found the place, got too close and the Jahangir put four into him."

Bridges lifted his hand. "Before you ask, he did not provide any intel on the house." He aimed the remote at the screen bringing up a picture of Mack outside the *Prater*.

"That leads me to your man, McMillan. I normally don't believe in coincidences. He accidentally picks Walters' scheduled rendezvous time *and* place to have a beer. He also looks a lot like Walters, same build, hair color, facial features. Siva didn't even question it. It's eerie.

"Luckily, McMillan is an exceptional man. He saved Siva Afari's life. There are not too many agents out there who would, self preservation being the rule."

"How do you know this?" Baxter asked.

"That's what you pay me to do." Bridges swallowed a mouthful of scotch waiting for Gunn to indicate whether he should continue. Gunn gave him a nearly imperceptible nod.

"McMillan killed the second in command of the Jahangir, which is good for us, bad for your man. Taher Zarif was a cold-blooded terrorist but his twin brother Tariq is a sick psychopath and a committed serial killer. You can be certain Tariq is desperate to kill McMillan to revenge his brother's death. That being said, McMillan is most likely safe until Tariq's role in the Iranian operation is over. *Most likely* being the operative words." Bridges raised his eyebrows.

"The Company and the Mossad have mobilized their top resources and set up command posts in Vienna. The target is the Agency, the IAEA. Your man McMillan stumbled into a terrorist plot and my guess is it's nuclear related."

"Should we get Mack out of Vienna?" Baxter asked. "We can send in one of the corporate jets and get him and his team of lawyers out. They were all coming back to the States on the Gulfstream on Thursday or Friday anyway."

Bridges said, "I don't think he'd go."

"What makes you think that?"

"Billy Mack, as you call him, has initiative. He broke into Siva Afari's rooftop apartment like he was James Bond. Inside, he subdued Tariq for a second time and left him unconscious. My gut tells me your Mack knows something.

"That's why he had the stones to go back to *Prater* and meet Siva knowing Farid and the Jahangir would have their guns pointed at him. He's ballsy, I'll say that. What I'd like to know is how he and her were allowed to just walk away. Tariq wasn't there but you can bet he was lurking nearby."

Baxter swallowed a healthy shot of his scotch. "Again, how do you know this?"

"I have a former operative in Vienna investigating Farid's mission. He's from my previous life in Iraq. My operative is a wild card with his own agenda but he had a source inside Iran feeding him solid intel. He learned the Assembly of Experts and the Ayatollah have green-lighted attacks in Washington and London. The Supreme Ruler of Iran doesn't green light run-of-the-mill terror attacks. This is war."

"War?" Baxter said. "C'mon."

"Why am I confident we're about to be at war? Because the only reason for the Ayatollah to send Farid to Vienna is to assure the weapons of mass destruction are delivered to the target cities. It's what he does. He delivers weapons to terror groups around the world. You add in the sick bastards of the Jahangir, Iran's junkyard dogs, and you've got a shit storm brewing." Bridges took a slow pull of scotch to let his words sink in. "Sources confirm the Jahangir is sending euphoric messages hailing their opportunity to be the ultimate suicide bombers who are about to bring the Great Satan to its knees.

"The final piece is the UN. It's logical to believe the IAEA and UN are unwitting dupes in this plot and Siva came across the evidence exposing the incompetence of the UN."

"Even the Iranians are not that crazy," Gunn said as he refilled Bridges' glass.

Bridges downed his glass. "The worldwide Caliphate has to start sometime, why not now? The Ayatollah has long promised the Caliphate in his lifetime and he's an old man."

Five minutes of awkward silence filled the room. For the past year, Gunn and Bridges had warned Baxter of the emergence of increased organized terror, funded and directed from Iran. Sources in the Middle East were telling Bridges of a plan being formulated inside Iran, the target was in the West with America as the likely prey. Baxter took the intel seriously and forwarded BIG's internal reports to Director of Intelligence at the CIA.

Baxter refilled everyone's glass as Bridges' prediction of a worldwide Caliphate was digested. If his book collection was any indication, Bridges was an expert on Middle Eastern history. He also knew the region's dusty, dirty streets having spent most of his career in the back alleys, the shops and questionable businesses in Iraq, Kurdistan and Syria. He knew how these people thought and how they acted.

"I pray to God you're wrong," Gunn said. To doubt Bridges about what to expect from the Mideast was a mistake Gunn had only made once. "If you are right, why do the Iranians care about Mack and Siva? I understand Tariq Zarif's interest in Mack, its revenge. But Farid?"

Bridges aimed the remote control at the screen. The video on the screen showed rows and rows of centrifuges then cut to three men kneeling on a dusty, dirty street outside a Mosque. "The answer to your question has two parts. First, the Iranians don't want the evidence Mack and Siva possess, whatever it is, to become public. It gives them plausible deniability. Second, there has been a rumor flying around for the past year of a list of Iranian spies deep inside the Department of Defense, CIA, FBI and get this, the White House. The Ayatollah is determined not to let that list get in the hands of anyone in the West. My source also tells me there is a second list floating around out there. It includes names of Iranians working to destroy Iran's nuclear program and bring down the Islamic Republic, and it's for sale."

Bridges sipped his drink and let his words sink in. "I think Billy Mack has both lists, whether he knows it or not. That doesn't matter because General Farid is convinced he and Siva have the lists."

"What do you recommend?" Gunn asked.

"Billy Mack was my favorite Major League player despite playing for the White Sox. Why? Because when he played, he was the best clutch player in the game. He always came through, always." For emphasis, Bridges downed the rest of his single malt. "I recommend you let him take his swings. He'll come through for you in the clutch."

"I hope you're right."

"Our time is getting short," Baxter said. "How familiar are you with S&H and their contract with the UN in Vienna?"

Bridges typed on his keyboard and an aerial view of the UN complex in Vienna popped on the screen. "S&H has provided basic security services to the entire UN in Vienna for fifteen years under two separate contracts, one for the IAEA and one for the rest of the UN. Six months ago, S&H bought Wiener Computer Logistics, a cyber security firm based in Vienna. Right after the acquisition closed, Wiener won a large bid to provide cyber security to the Agency. For obvious reasons, the IAEA's cyber security is managed separately from the other UN departments."

"How well do you know S&H as a company?" Baxter asked.

"I know S&H well and have some good contacts inside. It's a good company. They basically provide your run-of-the-mill corporate security and their clients are loyal, sticking with them for years. S&H is a good acquisition. I do have some reservations about Sunden Capital, the private equity firm selling S&H. It's owned by J Otis Weil. I ran into the man a few times in Damascus and Cyprus. My skin crawled after I shook hands with him. As soon as he let go of my hand, I checked for my wallet and watch."

"What are you saying?"

"Proceed with Caution. J Otis is a sociopath. He's like poison ivy on your privates."

CHAPTER 14

Mack and Siva sprinted onto the train platform just as the conductor blew his whistle twice. Dressed in a sharp blue uniform, the conductor waited for Siva to climb up before he waved his reflector wand to the engineer, signaling for the train to depart. Mack stepped up as the train started to move and nearly lost his grip. The conductor watched with a humorous look on his face.

Siva found an empty row in the back of the last car and took the seat on the aisle. Mack stepped over her to the window seat. Across the train yard two tired looking trains slowly chugged into the station.

Mack called the cheap flip phone he'd given

General Farid and gave him the decryption code for the USB device marked with an A. He repeated the code and hung up.

"Where are we going?" Siva asked, holding her phone in her hand.

"Bad Vöslau, about thirty minutes south." He held his hand out for Siva to hand him the phone. "Nobody needs to know where you are or where you're going. Give me your phone."

Siva dropped the phone in her purse and zipped it shut. "Why are we going to Bad Vöslau? Are we going to relax in a hot salt bath and drink wine?"

"Maybe next time. I have friends there and we can use some time to catch our breath."

"What if we are followed? Are you willing to put your friends in danger?"

Mack didn't have a quick answer. Nobody could have boarded the train after them. On the off chance anyone saw them board the train, they would only know it was headed south and the destination could be anywhere from Vienna to Graz, a city near the border with Slovenia.

"If I thought..." Mack didn't like the answer he was about to give and studied the workaday façades of the old buildings as the train rolled passed. The districts of Vienna surrounding the ornate, historic city center were blue-collar enclaves with mundane houses and apartments for the workers serving those who own and run the city.

"I wouldn't be going if I thought it was dangerous. When we arrive, I will explain to Rainer about our conversation with the General and he can decide if we stay or go."

Siva removed her sunglasses. "Do you trust this Rainer?"

"He's been my best friend since we were sixteen. He was an exchange student in high school and lived at my house for that year. He came back every summer. He's family."

It was Siva's turn to gaze out the window.

"*Fahrschein, bitte,*" the conductor said without taking his eyes off Siva. She paid for two tickets to Bad Vöslau and politely answered the conductor's questions, which were too many for Mack's liking, even if he didn't understand German.

Handing Mack his ticket, Siva said, "He wanted to know if you did this to my face. I told him no."

As the train hit it's cruising speed, conversations slowly faded giving way to the beat of the metal wheels clacking over the tracks. A light rain streaked along the windows.

"Who is the woman in the silver picture frame you have in your old display case?" Mack asked in a monotone intended to disarm and fluster Siva.

"She is-" Siva's entire body went rigid. Over the next minute, bewildered and bemused gave way to angry and annoyed. "You had better have a damn good reason for being in my apartment."

Mack felt no guilt. "I went to talk to you and when I arrived, there was blood on your door. That was a good enough reason for me."

Siva brought her fingers to her nose. "How did

you get in? The door and the frame are solid steel."

Mack explained his James Bond exploits, playing down the jump across the gap to the balcony and making no mention of crashing into the metal table and chair. He filled in the remainder of the story, glossing over the confrontation with Tariq as if it were no big deal. When he finished, he exhaled like he was exhausted, then asked, "Who is the woman in the silver picture frame?"

Siva angrily yanked the zipper open and dug into her purse, removing her leather wallet. She jerked the black leather snap from its clip and flipped it open to a clear plastic sleeve, turning it for Mack to see. Inside the sleeve was a picture of same beautiful woman from the video. She wore the same headscarf as when she led the Ayatollah.

"She is my sister. Her name is Zoya."

"Where does she live?"

"She lives here in Vienna and works at the UN. Actually, she works for the Agency."

"In the picture in your apartment she is standing in front of a large Mosque."

"That is the Fatima al-Masumeh Shrine in Qom, Iran. She lived there before moving to Vienna."

Mack kept his eyes on the picture. "I thought Qom was closed to Westerners. Not only for religious reasons but because the Fordow uranium enrichment center is located there."

"How do you know this about Qom?"

"I read. So, what's your sister's story?"

Annoyed, Siva said, "She was married to an Iranian she met while she studied at the University

College of London. Technically, they are still married. Karim, that's his name, was a diplomat at the London Embassy. They had a happy marriage living in London where she gave birth to two daughters. After the second girl was born, Karim's father, a powerful man inside Iran, made arrangements for Karim to be named Vice Mayor of Qom, a position created specifically for Karim.

"Once they were in Qom, Karim arranged for Zoya to work with the government where she could use her physics degree. Karim was a rising star in Iranian politics and as his popularity grew, he *evolved* into a hardcore follower of Sharia law and began treating Zoya and their two girls as goods and chattels, especially in public. When he started beating her, Zoya tried to begin divorce proceedings. It is virtually impossible for a woman to divorce her husband in Iran if the husband does not want the divorce. Zoya was very smart. From the day she started working, she began collecting sensitive evidence on the true nature of Iran's nuclear program. After she'd had enough of Karim's abuse, Zoya sat Karim's father down and explained how his son's bright future in Iranian politics would end if the true aim of the nuclear program was made public by his wife. Zoya and the father struck a deal. She would move to Vienna and work at the IAEA, the evidence would not see the light of day and they would have joint custody of their girls."

"How long have she and her daughters lived in Vienna?" Mack asked, nearly whispering.

"Funny you should ask." Siva's attention drifted out the window. Puddles formed under her eyes as she fought the urge to cry. She brushed her finger across each eye.

Mack gave her all the time she needed. Siva patted Mack's hand as if he was the one needing reassurance.

"The daughters were never allowed to leave Iran. Zoya came to Vienna to find an apartment and was not permitted to return to Iran. Karim's father paid her a visit one night to explain the new arrangement. Zoya could keep her job in Vienna, if the evidence Zoya collected ever became public, Zoya's daughters would be killed first, then after Zoya grieved for them, Zoya would be killed. That meant the daughters would stay in Qom and be raised by their new mother. Zoya had no choice but to accept."

"She must have legal rights she can pursue?"

"We are talking about Iran and she's a woman." Desperate to change the subject, Siva asked, "What does your friend Rainer do for a living?"

"I really don't know. He has some type of management consulting practice. He travels around the world on consulting assignments for international corporations and government agencies, working a week in one place, two weeks in another place. He doesn't seem to have a set schedule."

The speaker above Siva and Mack announced the train's arrival in Bad Vöslau.

Rainer stood at the end of the platform holding a large black umbrella above him and his daughter Anna. She was jumping up and down in anticipation.

CHAPTER 15

As soon as Mack stepped off the train and onto the platform, Anna was running toward him. Her long brown hair ended halfway down her back and bounced with each step. She had the exuberant smile, excited blue eyes of a child and the grace of a soon to be young woman. She was twelve.

"Uncle Billy," she said in English and eagerly gave him a genuine, unaffected hug. She released her arms and stepped back, like a soon-to-be teenager showing her independence.

"Thank you Anna, your hug made my day," Mack said.

Anna didn't fully understand his English but

Mack's smile translated everything she needed to know.

"This is my friend Siva," he said. "Siva, this is my Goddaughter, Anna."

Siva offered her hand and said in German, "My name is Siva and it is very nice to meet you, Anna."

Anna took a frightened step back. "What happened to your face?" she asked in German.

Siva crouched down and replied in German. "I was hit by a very bad man but I am fine. The bruises will heal."

Anna glared at Mack.

Siva took Anna's hand in hers. "It was not your Uncle Billy who did this. He is the man who rescued me."

As Anna and Siva chatted in German, Rainer bear hugged Mack, shook his hand and bear hugged him again. "Great to see you Billy. It's been too long."

"Way too long, over four years," Mack replied. "Let me introduce you to Siva then we should get out of this rain. We can do our catching up over a glass of wine, one of your better bottles."

The drive from the station to Rainer's house located on the edge of Bad Vöslau took five minutes. The entrance to the driveway was hidden from the street. After the automatic gate slid open, Rainer stopped with the back tires blocking the sensor so the gate wouldn't slide back shut.

"Is something wrong?" Mack asked.

Rainer didn't answer right away. His eyes were going through a routine, looking at four spots on the street in the same order. "Did you tell anybody where you were going?"

"No, and we hopped on the train while it was it was moving so nobody could have followed us."

Rainer nodded, checked the car's review mirror twice and drove down a long, narrow dirt path curving through thickets of trees. Coming around the third curve, a large lawn leading to a sizable stone house came into view. A tall wooden fence topped with spikes bordered the manicured yard. The yard was lit with motion sensor floodlights.

Bettina and Henri, Rainer's wife and son, stood in the doorway looking stern. As Mack approached, neither could hold the stony facade and together burst out laughing.

After extended hugs, introductions and small talk, Bettina led the way to the large Austrian kitchen. Mack remembered how important the kitchen was to Austrian socializing. In the middle of the table Bettina had laid out a platter of sliced meats and cheeses, pickles, olives, carrot sticks, sliced red peppers, a tub of *Liptauer* spicy cheese spread and three different types of bread.

Rainer disappeared down the steps and returned with two bottles of red wine, one in each hand. He held up his left hand. "Vega Unico?" then held up his right hand. "Or Petrus Pomerol?"

Mack shrugged his shoulders.

"Vega Unico," Siva said. "It's my favorite."

Rainer poured the wine around the table as Anna, too timid to speak English, peppered Mack with questions in German. Siva patiently translated. Every time Anna, Henri or Bettina giggled, Mack was certain Siva's translation included an added commentary.

After dinner was consumed and Anna ran out of questions, Rainer filled his and Mack's glass. "Let's go to my office, I have some things you should see."

"Papa," Anna said, "May I go to Sonja's house? Today is her birthday and her mother is having cake."

"No, we have guests," Rainer said sternly and watched Anna wilt in disappointment.

"But Papa, it stopped raining so Hildy is coming over to pick me up and all my friends are going," she said ready to burst into tears.

"How can you let her miss cake?" Mack said and Siva translated for Anna's benefit.

"OK, you can go, but only for one hour."

Anna hugged Mack then Siva and hurried to her room to change.

Henri pushed away from the table and removed his phone from his pocket. "May I be excused?"

Rainer nodded. "He's sixteen and in love. That means he'll be on the phone for the next hour or two."

Rainer grasped his wine glass. "Will you excuse us ladies? I want to show Billy my office."

The windows in Rainer's office overlooked the winding driveway and the manicured yard. On the wall left of the windows was a bank of black and white monitors showing camera feeds from every angle around the property. A large television hung on the opposite wall. On Rainer's desk was a large iMac and a white keyboard. Behind the desk was a heavy door with an industrial deadbolt lock. In the corner stood a gun safe, its door cracked open.

"While you're in my house, put that Glock you're

carrying into my gun safe."

Mack's mind spun as he laid the pistol on the top shelf. He decided not to ask how he knew.

Rainer plopped down on the leather sofa underneath the windows, spilling a drop of wine on his hand. He licked it off. "Have you told me everything about your adventure in the *Prater*? Sometimes we forget an important detail like why you're carrying."

"There isn't more to tell. I have to watch my back for the psychopath whose brother I killed and whose gun I have."

Mack changed the subject. "This is quite an operation you have here," he said, tapping the window with his finger. "Bulletproof glass and a security system to rival Fort Knox."

"My clients require discretion."

"You know, you've never really explained what you do."

Rainer cleared his throat contemplating his response. "I provide advice on industrial espionage, helping companies and organizations protect themselves from each other. Knowledge is the new gold. Whoever owns the knowledge owns the world."

"Interesting perspective but I'm not convinced."

"Think about it. Say you develop a new, groundbreaking product and before you can manufacture it, the Russians or the Chinese hack into your system, steal your proprietary information and start manufacturing it before you do. You've just lost millions, perhaps billions. For some countries, it is easier and cheaper to steal ideas and products then develop them.

It's the world we're living in."

Rainer grinned in a way to let Mack know he was done talking about his work. "Tell me about Siva. This is the woman who walked up to you in the *Prater*? She's gorgeous, smart and has great taste in wine."

Mack described Siva's walk toward him and how she seemed reluctant to sit. He skipped ahead to finding the USB device in his pocket and explained the photos and videos on the USB devices but didn't go into the embedded clues Nimesh and Susan Baisley had found. He described General Farid without mentioning the repeated death threats from the earlier *Prater* encounter.

Rainer walked over to his desk, turned on his iMac and typed in his log-in information. "What are you going to do about this psychopath?" he asked as he waited for the computer to come to life.

"I don't know. I'm kind of playing it as it goes along." Mack held up his wine glass and frowned as if to say *what else can I do?*

A young girl's bone-chilling screams reverberated up the steps.

"That's Anna's voice," Rainer said as he flew down the steps three at a time. Mack was right behind him, closer than his shadow.

CHAPTER 16

Rainer and Mack sprinted down the steps and into the foyer to find the front door wide open. Rainer grabbed Mack's arm, told him to stay put and sprinted back up the steps. He returned with two Beretta M9s and handed one to Mack. Mack stuck the gun in his waistband and pulled out his shirttail as cover. Rainer followed suit.

Siva and Bettina were in the front yard helping Anna's friend Hildy to her feet. Hildy's lip was swollen and bleeding and she needed help staying on her feet.

Siva brushed the hair from Hildy's thin face, calmly asking her where Anna was. Hildy burst out crying and pointed down the long path running through a thick patch of trees.

"We opened the gate and two men took her," Hildy said between sobs. "The big one hit Anna and lifted her up. When Anna screamed the man put a gun here." She made a gun with her thumb and index finger and held it to her temple.

Rainer translated Hildy's words to Mack then sprinted through the gate and down the dark path. "The street is a hundred meters down this path." His words trailed off when he hit the path.

Mack caught up halfway down the path, staying a step behind Rainer.

Two gunshots rang out ahead of them. Rainer froze. Mack sprinted passed him, slowing as he come to the street. A single street lamp illuminated the entrance to the park across the street. The street was empty except for a Volvo station wagon parked down the street with its motor running and tailgate up.

Mack stayed in the shadows until Rainer caught up.

"We have a car down the street with its motor running," Mack said, discreetly pointing to his left. "Make your way toward the car and stay out of sight. I will circle around the right and come in from the woods on the other side."

Rainer nodded and slipped into the darkness behind the trees.

Mack took a wide line, crouching when he was in open ground and sprinting when the park was not visible. Coming into the park, he used the low hanging branches of the numerous old oak trees as cover. He sidestepped his way across the grass until he saw the silhouette of a man standing next to a thick wooden picnic table. Hanging in his right hand was a long handgun, a Colt six-shooter. He stood over a body.

Mack stayed in the shadows, moving like a panther stalking its prey. Ten feet from the man, Mack raised the Beretta to eye level. "Keep your hands where I can see them."

The man took a big step back and spread his hands away from his body, the Colt hanging from his index finger.

"Please Mr. John Wayne not to shoot me," Shah said and turned to face Mack, his humor intended to disarm while his eyes pleaded for restraint. He flicked his head for Mack to look to his right. On the other side of the picnic table, lay the body of a young man with long black hair and thick black beard. "He is Jahangir."

Rainer marched up from behind Shah with his Beretta pointed at Shah's head.

"He's alright Rainer."

Mack rolled the body over. Blood pumped from two bullet holes on each side of his chest. The man gurgled trying to say something, coughed up blood and began choking. Mack walked over to Shah.

"Put your gun on the table and sit." Mack pointed his pistol at the picnic table. "You have some explaining to do."

There was neither joy nor regret in Shah. Keeping his hands out wide, he walked over to the dying man and put his hand over his mouth and nose, cutting off his air supply. He pressed down until the man jerked twice and went limp.

"That was more human, if that is right word, than Faruk deserve."

"Humane," Mack said, watching Shah close the dead man's eyes. "I want an explanation for why you are here."

Shah wiped the blood from his hand on Faruk's lifeless pants, strolled over and sat on the picnic table bench. "I came to here because I think you maybe need taxi back to city."

"How did you know where we were?" Mack asked. He slid Shah's gun out of reach.

"I hear you tell the beautiful woman where you to go when I driving you to *Hauptbahnhof*. I hurry to beat train here and see you coming out. I think when you call for ride, I be here. Then I see Tariq and this man he called Faruk outside fence and I follow. I going to front gate to tell you of these Jahangir outside fence when I hear scream and I see big man Tariq carrying girl to white van. He give her to a man in back of van and shut door then make telephone call talking in Persian. I hear him say he deliver girl back to house in thirty minutes. After he off telephone, I try stop him." He nudged Faruk's dead body with his foot. "This Faruk come at me and grabbing for gun. I shoot him but he keep coming so I shoot him again. I want to shoot Tariq but he in van and driving away." Shah handed Mack a cheap phone. "This was telephone he use. He drop on ground."

Mack wasn't sure how much to believe but Shah was very convincing. He removed the Beretta from his waistband and placed it on the table to intimidate Shah. A strange feeling ate at Mack's gut. Shah was probably lying or at least deceiving by not telling the whole story. Part of him wanted to believe Shah's white lies. The other part wanted to shake the truth out of him. "Now I want the real story," he said, spinning the Beretta.

Shah didn't blink. He was in no hurry to answer, content in his thoughts.

"This is what I must do," he finally said. "I made promise to my wife back at my home in Mahabad before she die of broken heart."

Siva's voice resounded clearly through the quiet night air. "Mack, Rainer, get back here, now." The word 'Now' cut through the trees and seemed to grow with more urgency as it approached.

Mack sprung to his feet, eyeing Shah's gun on the picnic table. "What are you going to do?" he asked.

"I put body in car and drive it to river then I come back to here. I think thirty minutes for me to come back. You will have telephone call over by time I back."

"Telephone call? How do you know there is a telephone call?"

"I know how Persians think. He will be Tariq calling to make trade for get revenge." Shah retrieved his gun off the table, stuck it in his pants behind him and lifted Faruk's body over his shoulder. He dumped the body in the back of the Volvo and waved to Mack.

Mack ran like it was the bottom of the ninth and he was rounding third coming home with the game winning run. Rainer was a step behind him.

Coming into the yard, Siva was on the phone speaking Persian.

She placed the phone against her chest while

Mack caught his breath.

When Mack nodded he was ready, Siva put the phone back to her ear and said, "Here he is."

Siva handed the phone to Mack. "It is Tariq Zarif. I believe you know him. He says he has Anna and will trade her for you. If you do not agree, he's threatening to make arrangements for her to be sent to a jihadist camp as a sex slave. They like their woman young."

Mack brought the phone up to his ear. He thought of Anna and caught himself before he lost his cool and ripped into Tariq telling him to go to hell. He stuck the phone against his chest.

The concern on Rainer's face eased a hair as Henri helped Bettina inside. Once the front door closed, Rainer's eyes narrowed and his face hardened. Mack had never seen this side of Rainer. There was no hate emanating from him, just agonizing determination. "Put the call on speaker," he said.

"I plan to." Mack replied matter-of-factly. He tapped the screen and handed the phone to Siva. "Tell him I agree to the trade on my terms, at a time and place of my choosing."

Siva translated, speaking rapidly into the phone and then listened intently. "He does not agree. He will determine where and when or Anna will never be seen again."

Mack snatched the phone from Siva's hand. "I know you understand English Tariq. I will tell you when and where the exchange takes place or I will call your boss, General Farid and tell him he will not receive the device and final code for the information he desperately

needs. When I tell him why, he will certainly kill you."
Mack hung up the phone.

"What the fuck are you doing?" Rainer screamed.

Siva added, "That man is a psychopath, Mack."

"Precisely, Tariq thinks he has the upper hand. Combine that with his fanatical lust for revenge and he'll call back. He needs to get this over with quickly. He still has General Farid's mission to complete." Mack lifted his arm and checked his watch. "Ten bucks say he'll call back within two minutes."

It took less than a minute for Siva's phone to ring. She checked the caller ID and handed the phone to Mack. "It's for you."

A smile grew on Mack's face listening to Tariq rant, promising him a slow and painful death. At the end of his tirade, Tariq agreed to Mack's terms.

When Tariq finished speaking, Mack silently counted off thirty-seconds on his watch. He could feel Tariq squirming as he waited for Mack to reply. Mack cleared his throat then waited another fifteen-seconds. It was an eternity to Tariq. Mack finally said, "I'm handing the phone to Siva so there is no confusion."

Siva simultaneously translated Mack's instructions into Persian. "There is a baseball field just off Prater Hauptallee, on the southwestern part of Prater Park. Be on the field at nine-thirty tomorrow morning, alone. At the same time, Anna is to be delivered to Siva outside the front entrance to the Opera House, the Staatsoper. When I receive a call from Siva, I will walk out on the field." Mack hung up and handed the phone to Siva.

"There is a baseball field in Vienna?" Siva asked.

"Yes, there is a baseball field in Vienna," Rainer answered. "I played at Prater Field for many seasons."

Mack had taught Rainer the game of baseball when he lived with Mack's family for sophomore year in high school and every summer he went back to visit. Mack was fond of telling him baseball was an individual team sport. Before each pitch every player had to anticipate the numerous outcomes and know his responsibilities for each. Mack wanted to lure Tariq onto a baseball field because he had a play in mind.

"What is your plan?" Siva asked.

"I will tell you when I get back." Mack strolled down the path. Before he was out of sight, he yelled, "I have someone to see first." He headed down the path to the park to see if Shah returned.

Rainer hurried down the path catching up to Mack as he came to the street. "These bastards took Anna, my daughter. I have the final say on any plan you're concocting."

"I know where Anna is being taken. Follow me." Mack walked across the street back into the park.

"How do you know that?"

"Shah overheard Tariq speaking on the phone."

Rainer stood at the end of the path, bothered by the ease in which Anna was taken and wondering why Tariq was calling so quickly. He ran to catch up to Mack.

"Wait a minute, Mack," Rainer said. He put his hand on Mack's shoulder and stepped in front, stopping him.

"Why did Tariq, a terrorist, call Siva's phone and how did he know she would be here at my house?"

CHAPTER 17

General Farid put on a plain sport coat, tweed trousers, a button down shirt and a striped tie. The mirror said he was dressed for the part, looking like a typical United Nations bureaucrat in everything but his demeanor. He slumped his shoulders to hide his military bearing. That was better. He would fit in at the UN. He worried about the Jahangir and their unwillingness to shave their beards.

He lit a cigarette and his mind drifted to his last major mission, the funding and arming the Islamic State of Iraq and Syria, or ISIS. Those fighters made the Jahangir look like a Boy Scout troop. With ISIS, there was less concern for secrecy and covert communication. The need for increased secrecy on this mission was due to the incompetence of the woman in charge. It's probably how the sensitive lists and mission instructions ended up in the hands of Siva Afari, a failure to be addressed after the mission.

Despite Tariq's antics, the operation was progressing due to the General's leadership. Decrypting the first USB device and deleting the videos and photos didn't take long. The decoding of the instructions embedded in the text took two hours. The first half of the mission was now laid out for him and the Jahangir.

The IAEA security ID badges along with fifty thousand Euros were in a locker at the *Hauptbahnhof.* Courier had delivered the locker key the day before. The badges gave unfettered access to the IAEA's offices in the Vienna International Center and to a separate nuclear storage facility secretly located five kilometers northeast, just outside the city limits. Papers authorizing the transfer of two specialty crates containing highly radioactive waste for decommissioning would be delivered separately.

The mission's transport was arranged. A van was modified to transport nuclear material and was parked in the IAEA parking garage on the third subfloor, stall number 317. The van had the IAEA identification sticker on the windshield and UN license plates. Security guards on duty wouldn't question the badges and the van. After the merchandise was unloaded, fifty grand for the security guards was to be left in the van.

General Farid and his team were to enter the main IAEA entrance and check-in with building security at precisely ten-thirty. At ten forty-five, the building's security cameras will experience a malfunction and all recordings will be erased. While the cameras are out, the team makes it's way to the parking garage via the main elevator. The van must be driven out of the facility within fifteen minutes. That's when the security cameras start working again.

The General committed the first part of the mission to memory and wished he had time to further train the Jahangir. They needed another dose of military discipline.

Thirsty, he stubbed out his cigarette on the carpet and went down to the kitchen to make tea.

Hamid, the quiet one, sat at the table reading the Koran. In his free time, Hamid always read the Koran. When the General walked in, Hamid stood. The General was pleased and smiled at him. Finally, one of the fanatics showed proper respect. He signaled for Hamid to sit back down.

General Farid filled the electric kettle with tap water and pushed the switch. He asked, "Where are Tariq and Faruk this evening?"

Hamid placed his bookmark in the crease, respectfully closed the book and laid it on the table. "They left together two hours ago. They did not tell me where they were going."

"Do they not know why we are here? If there is a mistake or a misstep, the mission will surely fail. If that happens, I will kill every Jahangir I see, including you Hamid."

"Then I will die a martyr for the Caliph."

The General rolled his eyes as he poured boiling

water over his tea bag.

There was a scuffle outside the kitchen followed by a young girl speaking rapidly in German. General Farid rushed to the foyer. Tariq stood just inside the front door holding a small girl wearing a black hood.

The General impulsively reached for his sidearm. If he didn't need every able body for the success of the mission, Tariq would be lying dead on the floor. The General knew that if the mission failed, he, Iran's greatest military mind would be called to Tehran and never be seen from again, all because of a fool named Tariq.

"What the hell are you doing and who the hell is this?"

"She is insurance. The American CIA agent, this Billy Mack, will do whatever we want to save this girl."

"You disobeyed my orders Tariq."

"When I talked to your boss, she liked my plan and she gave me orders to take the girl and trade her for some kind of important list the American CIA agent has."

Calling a woman *his boss* was another unforgivable insult. General Farid again fought the urge to kill Tariq there and then. He reminded himself the operation took precedent. After the mission, he would behead Tariq and force his family to keep his head on a stake outside their house.

"Where is Faruk?"

Tariq lied, "I don't know."

"You and Faruk left the house together. Did he tell you where he was going?"

"No, he received a call and left in a hurry."

The General became suspicious. The use of

phones while at the safe house was strictly prohibited. "Who knows Faruk is in Vienna?"

"The woman who is your boss, your superior." Tariq said. He twitched, wanting to smile.

General Farid grabbed Tariq by the throat and slammed him up against the wall. "I do not report to a woman. I have no superior, especially not a woman. Women are for the kitchen and the bedroom. That is something you wouldn't know." He shoved Tariq out the door.

"Hamid, follow me," General Farid said and lifted Anna. He carried her down the steps to the basement giving instructions to Hamid as he went.

While Hamid removed the black hood from Anna's head and tied her hands and legs, General Farid checked on the woman cowering in the corner. She called herself Karin.

"You better hope your boyfriend follows instructions."

"I keep telling you I don't have a boyfriend." Seeing Anna tied to the wall, a rage tore through Karin. "You're a fucking animal. She's a little girl."

The General slapped her hard nearly breaking her jaw. "Don't say another word, either of you," he said in German.

Anna burst into a crying fit and dropped her chin to hide her face.

General Farid yanked her chin up and raised his right hand. "If you cry, I will give you something to cry about." He held his hand over her until she sniffed long and slow and her breathing returned to a semblance of normal.

He climbed the steps with one thought in mind. After the mission was over, he would use Tariq for target practice.

CHAPTER 18

Standing on the street outside the park, Rainer's question continued to ring in Mack's ears. *Why would Tariq call Siva's phone?* The question gave way to a more dangerous question. How did Tariq and Faruk know he and Siva were at Rainer's house?

There was one person who may have the answer. Odds were in his favor Shah would return to the park after dumping the body.

"One trip around the park and only one. If he's not here, he isn't coming back," Mack said.

Mack and Rainer entered the park to find Shah sitting on top the picnic table with his feet on the bench, smoking a cigarette.

"Mr. John Wayne, you believe when I tell to you I come back." Shah smiled but there was no joy behind it.

Mack climbed onto the picnic table and sat close to Shah. "Why are you in Vienna?"

"Why was little girl taken?"

"I have something they want and Tariq wants to kill me to revenge his brother. He will trade her for me. Now, why are you in Vienna?"

Shah sucked in a long drag off his cigarette, exhaled the smoke over his head and watched it dissipate into the dark sky.

"I am here as promise to my wife before she die. I come here to kill three men and now there are two left." A small wisp of smoke curled out his nose.

"You killed a man here in Vienna?" Mack asked.

"No Mr. John Wayne, I did not." Shah flicked his cigarette butt toward the streetlight. "You kill him ... at *Prater*."

"Taher Zarif?" Mack said the name like he was just kicked in the crotch. One of the skills Mack prided himself on was his ability to anticipate. Playing baseball he learned the importance of anticipating, knowing what would happen when the ball was put in play and he successfully carried that skill over to his business career.

No matter how skilled he was, Mack would never have anticipated Shah's answer. He gathered his wits. "Who are the other two?" he asked, knowing the answer. "And why are you going to kill them?" He didn't know the answer to that question.

"General Hafez Farid and Taher Zarif's brother, Tariq Zarif." Shah lit another cigarette to calm himself.

He studied the burning end of the cigarette seemingly lost in thought. He slowly turned his head.

"My son was working as engineer in Qom. He come home to Mahabad every weekend to visit his mother. She was sick many years with bad heart." Shah tapped the center of his chest. Cigarette ash fell onto his pants. "One weekend my son not come home. We not hear from him for many weeks. A friend from his workings come to house and show us video. My son was praying in Mosque when General Hafez Farid and two Zarif take him outside." A tear rolled down his cheek. "Tariq Zarif call my son a spy for Mossad. My son never do spying for Mossad. He not ever spy for Mossad, not ever." Shah spat on the ground. "Tariq Zarif make up lie. General Farid hu ... hum ... make fool of my son. Then he shoot him six times. When my wife see shooting of son she die of broken heart. Before she die, I promise to her I kill General Farid and Zarif brothers."

"How did you know General Farid was in Vienna?"

"I am knowing some people."

"Do you know where General Farid and Tariq Zarif are staying in Vienna?"

"They have house in *neunzehnte Bezirk*, I do not know words in English. The house have many guarders. First time I go pretending I get taxi call. They put gun in face and tell me leave. It is big house, many openings."

Shah fumbled through his pockets for his pack of cigarettes until he realized he had a lit cigarette in his mouth.

"Just a second," Mack said, holding up his finger.

He walked into the shadows with Rainer.

In a low voice, Mack said, "I'm going to ask Shah to show up at the Prater baseball field tomorrow morning instead of me. If I'm right, it will be a surprise and throw off Tariq. It could give Shah a shot at Tariq."

"What makes you think Tariq will show up and not some other terrorist?"

"He is bent on revenge and has to pull the trigger himself. If Tariq doesn't show and sends a surrogate, we still eliminate a terrorist."

Rainer studied the silhouette of Shah sitting atop the picnic table with a lone streetlight behind him. "You have nothing to lose and Shah would jump at the chance. There is a downside though. If it is an ambush, you would be sending Shah to his death."

"True." Mack climbed back up on the picnic table and explained to Shah the agreement he made earlier with Tariq for the *trade* at Prater's baseball field, twice repeating the high probability of it being an ambush.

Shah didn't wait to be asked. "I be there."

Rainer sat on the other side of Shah. "How do you think Tariq knew Siva and Mack were here?"

Shah studied his cigarette thinking of his answer. "Maybe sticking something in Siva bag but I only guessing."

"I'll call you," Mack said. He and Rainer left Shah sitting on the picnic table smoking his cigarette. A melancholy calm had come over Shah as if he were on a journey.

Back at the house, Siva and Bettina sat in the kitchen with the evening's dirty dishes still in front of them.

Bettina's hands shook and tears welled in her eyes. Rainer whispered in her ear and her hands steadied.

The question of why Tariq called Siva's phone was foremost in Mack's mind. Asking Siva this question had only one outcome — bad. No matter how much it upset Siva, the answer would go a long way to learning how Tariq knew where they were. Mack decided to get it over with. Gotta do whatcha gotta do.

"Siva, why do you think Tariq called your phone to arrange the trade for Anna?"

Siva stroked her chin before her shoulders tensed and her brown eyes hardened. "I hope you are not accusing me of being complicit with those animals."

Mack leaned back like he was surprised at her answer. It was a tactic he successfully used in his business dealings. "Of course not. If we know why he called your phone, we can figure out how Tariq knew we were here and why Anna was targeted." Mack always used 'we' instead of 'I' in situations like this, as if everyone was on the same team.

Mack could see Siva was counting to ten. He added, "Look, we believe you. We are concerned with how Tariq found us."

Siva's shoulders relaxed. "I have no idea why he called me. I only saw that animal at *Prater* when he grabbed me and you came to the rescue and then in the basement of some house when he did *this* to me." She turned her head for Mack to get a better look at her black eye. "Both times he demanded I give him the USB devices or he'd kill me."

"You can understand why I had to ask. The optics are not in your favor. You live in a penthouse apartment and work at the UN, you-"

"The apartment belongs to my parents, which is no business of yours."

"Are you the only one using your phone?" Rainer asked, hoping to change the subject.

"Of course, I always have it with me."

"Don't be so quick to answer. Think back. Did you ever leave it somewhere, get it repaired, lose it for a short period of time?"

Siva stroked her chin again. "No, I've had it with me since I bought it. The only person to ever use it was my sister and that was six months ago when she first moved here." Siva squeezed her eyes closed. When she opened them, she added, "When I was in the basement, those animals took my bag but my phone was off at the time."

Mack pulled out his own phone and called Nimesh. The call was answered on the first ring.

"Where the hell you been, Mack? I've been trying to contact you for the last twenty-four hours."

"I'll tell you later. How good are you at hacking a person's cellphone?"

"I just hired a new whizkid. He's a magician. Let me get him." Nimesh texted Jonah Klein to come to his office. "Mack, your bosses have called me every thirty minutes and are on their way to my office. I've never seen them this worried."

"They are next on my to-call list. Do me a big favor and don't tell them about this conversation. I'm going to ask you to do me a big favor and no one needs to know about it."

"You're putting me in a tough spot, Mack. Baxter is already pissed at you for not answering your phone."

"Trust me, this is much more important than my boss being pissed at me. I'll tell him in due time."

Jonah Klein strolled into the office dressed like a high school student. Nimesh gestured for him to close the door. He put the phone on speaker. "I have Jonah Klein with me."

Mack said, "Jonah, can you hack a cellphone?"

"Yes, how long it takes depends on the phone."

"What if you have the access code?"

"That's not hacking, it's just accessing."

"I want you to see if you can find any type of tracking device or tracking code on the phone."

"Easier than winning Super Mario Bros. Give me the number and the code."

Siva reluctantly gave the number and her access code.

No one said a word while Jonah typed away. Siva went to the kitchen to get a bottle of water. Before she put it in her mouth, she gave Mack a hard look, like she was being violated.

Klein broke her concentration. "Someone programmed the phone to ping cell towers every five minutes and triangulate the phones position. Do you want me to turn it off?"

"Yes," Siva said forcefully.

"No," Mack said more forcefully.

CHAPTER 19

In Washington, just north of the White House, Baxter ordered the limo driver to circle Farragut Square, turn onto K Street and pull over in front of the first building. The driver received his instructions and when the door slammed shut, sped away. Gunn and Baxter strolled into an office building like they were heading to a meeting.

Gunn punched the touch screen directory a number of times as if he were checking for a name. "We have the wrong address," he said loudly and followed Baxter outside. They cut through Farragut Square, doubled back to check for a tail and crossed the street. Around the corner, they slipped into a small falafel shop with two tables in a small back room. The man behind the counter nodded to Gunn.

Gunn found the door disguised as part of the red paneled wall and led Baxter up a narrow staircase. On the next level, a cramped hallway led to a cheap door with a rusty 'Men's Room' sign screwed into it. He knocked twice on a hollow birch door and turned the handle. A security guard big enough to play tackle in the NFL stood in their way. He recognized Gunn and stepped aside.

At a table across the low-ceilinged room sat a deeply tanned man wearing a dark suit and French-cuffed shirt. His thick salt and pepper hair was combed back ending at the nape of his neck. Next to him was a lithesome, sandy-haired woman dressed in a form-fitting blue dress. Her hair was pulled back and swirled into a bun.

Baxter recognized the newly appointed Director of Intelligence for the CIA from news reports.

Baxter and Gunn sat across from the spooks. Gunn made the introductions. "Sam, this is Samantha Stern, the Director of Intelligence and you know David Countryman. He's just been named Deputy Director of the National Clandestine Service." No handshakes were offered or expected.

The man working the counter downstairs placed a large plate of hummus and unleavened bread in the center then sat at the end of the table.

"This is Javeed," Samantha said. Baxter and Gunn knew it wasn't his real name. "He is Iranian and a valuable source of intelligence here and in Iran. Lately, he's been spending most of his time here. Ironically, here in the heart of the nation's capital there is a large contingent of radical young Muslims planning to attack us. Javeed has infiltrated the inner circle."

"I am an Iranian born Kurd," Javeed said. "I am one of the millions of Kurds with the misfortune of being born in Iran." He dipped a piece of bread in the hummus and took his time chewing.

Baxter said, "There'll be another time to discuss your bio or your motivation. We were told you had information affecting our man in Vienna."

"I know nothing of your man in Vienna. My source is in Qom. He is from my hometown of Mahabad in Iranian Kurdistan near the Iraqi border."

Countryman said, "Javeed's source inside the Iranian government works in Research Division of the Atomic Energy Organization of Iran."

"He worked at the Fordow facility outside Qom. He was killed by the Republican Guard a month ago. He was my cousin and when I saw him last in Mahabad, he told me of Iran's plan to start a war with the Americans and British. The attacks will be on American and British soil and be simultaneous. Inside the facility he worked, he overheard senior officials bragging at how surprised the West would be."

"When did he tell you this?" Gunn asked.

"Three months ago, when I was home for a visit."

"It could be just bluster, government officials talking big like they are in the know," Gunn said.

Javeed was shaking his head before Gunn finished speaking. "My cousin was very worried. The Fordow facility has been on lock-down for six months. No visitors are allowed in and employee access inside the facility has been severely restricted. Security throughout the plant has been doubled."

Javeed dipped another piece of bread in the hummus and chewed slowly.

"Has this been reported up the chain?" Baxter asked.

Samantha Stern leaned forward resting her elbows on the table. "We've sent the intel reports to the White House but the twits around the President have watered down the information and downplayed the threat. We have it on good account the IAEA is altering the inspection reports on Iran's nuclear development to reflect a decrease in the uranium enrichment program. This deliberate deception contradicts our sources who tell us Iran has already enriched enough uranium to fuel two small nuclear weapons."

Javeed pushed the plate of hummus to Baxter. "You must try this, it is the best hummus you will ever have."

Watching Baxter dip the bread, Javeed said, "Here in Washington, the young radical Muslims are constantly talking about how they are going to rip out the heart of the Great Satan and lead the coming of the Caliphate. They love to talk big and they routinely spill sensitive information."

Baxter said, "Young radicals always talk big."

Javeed said, "For the last month, maybe six weeks, the most vocal and radical self-proclaimed Mujahideen have gone silent. The leaders have spent an inordinate amount of time together inside the Mosque. In my five years of praying at that Mosque, this has never happened. Before and after prayers, the more fervent radicals wanting to join the leadership are bragging of a great day coming soon."

Samantha crossed her legs and her arms. "Our analysts have noticed a significant drop in signals communications from the various terror organizations lately. It's as if they were ordered to go radio silent."

Countryman said, "This runs counter to our experience. Whenever a terror attack is planned, the chatter increases dramatically. To go as quiet as they have is a likely indication of something big."

"What are your analysts telling you?" Gunn asked.

"Our top analysts are all over the board. Since the White House is not taking this seriously, some of our senior analysts are letting politics dictate their reports and have watered down the intelligence. It gives the White House further justification for their inaction."

Countryman said, "My sources are convinced this attack will be 9-11 times ten, a hundred thousand dead, minimum."

"You both have been very generous outsourcing sensitive operations to BIG in the past. What can we do to assist you with this?" Baxter asked.

Those words were music to the ears of Samantha and Countryman. Countryman dipped a piece of bread in the hummus and popped it in his mouth, as if rewarding himself.

"Given the Administration's position on this, we can't authorize any government-sponsored covert action," Samantha said. "If you, as a contract service provider to the Agency, can provide assistance to our counter-terrorism operations in Europe, starting with our office and operations in Vienna, we would welcome your efforts."

"We will provide you with the same high quality service you are used to getting from BIG Security and Defense," Baxter said. "When do we start?"

"Yesterday," Samantha said. She and Javeed stared at each other. Samantha gestured with her fingers as if to tell Javeed *give it to me.*

Javeed handed over a flimsy five-by-eight photograph. Samantha looked it over like she was authenticating it before placing it in front of Baxter and Gunn.

Javeed tapped the picture. "This photo was given to me by my cousin when I was home. I have been trying to reach him for a month to ask him more about this picture but he hasn't answered his phone or replied to my emails. That is the Ayatollah and the Assembly of Experts touring the Fordow nuclear facility, specifically its uranium enrichment facility." Javeed tapped the picture again, near the face of a woman wearing a headscarf. "According to my cousin, this woman is responsible for getting two nuclear bombs into Vienna and then to America and England. My cousin works in her department and has not seen her at the Fordow facility for over six months. Her name is Zoya Afari. Her husband is a rising political star in Iran and the most fervent supporter of starting World War III with the West."

Stern added, "We want this threat wrapped up in

Vienna neatly and cleanly. If your people screw up, we disavow any knowledge and all contracts with BIG end up in a burn bag."

Baxter followed Gunn out the falafel shop by the back exit, down a makeshift hall and through a metal door into a stairwell. At the bottom of the stairs, Gunn tapped a code into a keypad next to the set of double doors. The door on the left clicked open. Gunn looked out the door, held up his arm to stop Baxter from exiting and took a step into the alley. The limo was waiting one door down. The driver miscounted.

The drive out of central Washington took them past the round dome of the Jefferson Memorial, across the Potomac River and around the Pentagon. The immensity of the Pentagon always astounded and intrigued Baxter. He had a standing offer with the Department of Defense to buy the building.

For the remainder of the trip, Baxter checked messages on his iPad and responded to only the most urgent. Gunn spent the entire trip engaged in a conference call with David Countryman and Casey Ryan, the CIA Station Chief in Vienna. Over a public line, Ryan was reticent to admit he had an agent in the field and had lost track of Mack. Plausible deniability.

Coming into Arlington, Virginia, the limo drove around and behind a plain, two-story, red brick building next to a strip mall. A small gold sign next to the bulletproof door read *Mira Labs*. There was no handle on the door only a small keypad to the left of where door handle would normally be found.

Mira Labs was the cyber security company founded by Nimesh. Baxter provided the seed capital in exchange for twenty-five percent ownership.

As Baxter and Gunn approached, the door swung open. Baxter waved to the pinhole camera hidden above the door.

A short, thin teenager with a smooth face greeted them inside the door. "I'm Jonah," he said, his voice hadn't dropped yet. Dressed in skinny jeans, Doc Martin shoes, a t-shirt and sweater vest, he looked like he was ready for his first day of high school. He led them to a conference room on the other side of the building.

Across the room, Nimesh sat with his feet up on the long conference table engaged in a video chat. He ended the call and met Baxter and Gunn midway across the room.

"I see you've met Jonah Klein. He's our newest member. We coaxed him to leave Princeton."

Responding to the disconcerted look on Baxter's face, Jonah said, "I'm older than I look. I turn twenty next month."

"Don't rush it kid," Baxter said, chuckling as he patted him on the shoulder. "Let's get this show on the road."

Jonah's fingers danced around his mini-tablet and two screens dropped from the ceiling. On the left screen was a live video call with Susan Baisley. Her hair hung loose and she wore her cat eyeglasses. On the right screen was a 3-D map of the world with thin red lines crisscrossing the map.

Jonah said, "The map represents the different

URLs used for all communications coming out of Iran's Fordow Nuclear facility and all government offices in and around Qom. I wrote an algorithm with specific criteria and kept narrowing the search." He tapped his tablet and the map melted away. A list of URLs and physical addresses appeared under four country headings, Austria, Iran, United Kingdom and United States.

"The first address in Austria is a cyber café near the University. The café's server is wiped clean every night and there are no public cameras anywhere in the vicinity so that's a bust. The other address is a house in the far northern part of the city. I piggybacked a satellite and have a photo of the house if you want to see it."

"It's the safe house Walters discovered before he was killed," Nimesh said. "I gave a call to Casey Ryan to request some eyes on the house but he needs a week to staff up."

Jonah said, "The three addresses in the US are the library at George Washington University, a cyber café in Georgetown and a bookstore near Dupont Circle."

"The cyber café is a hangout for young Muslims," Susan Baisley added. "We have hours and hours of video footage outside the café and have identified a number of known radicals. There is no way to connect anyone with any computer usage inside. We have been able to download every email sent from the café's router as well as a list of the websites visited. Take a look at this email trail we found."

Stacked emails appeared on the screen on the right.

"What can you conclude from the emails?" Baxter

asked.

"Basically, the terrorists in Washington are sending and receiving emails, other social media messages confirming the preparations are complete, and providing an accounting of the cash needed."

Jonah clicked the mouse and an email message came on the screen for everyone to read.

Susan said, "Before you ask, there is no mention of any specific date or any timing, just the money amounts. We have tagged the Iranian banks and the secret government accounts. Once the cash starts flowing from the Iranian accounts into the US and UK, the attacks will soon follow. That's the best I can give you."

"We do have some good news," Nimesh said and winked at Jonah. "Jonah has done something even the Mossad has been unable to do. He's hacked into the main server of the Atomic Energy Organization of Iran."

Jonah acted like it was no big deal. "It's not as propitious as I was hoping. The facilities for enriching uranium are no longer on-line. Fordow went off-line a week ago. All activity on the server is now consistent with normal bureaucratic operations. I will need more time to wiggle my way into the other facilities."

Gunn leaned close to Nimesh. "Propitious?"

Nimesh shrugged his shoulders. "He's one of those Big Bang geniuses."

"What do you conclude from the evidence we've seen?" Baxter asked.

Nimesh said, "I think I can speak for all us." Susan and Jonah nodded grimly.

"An attack is coming soon, very soon. It is not

going to be a typical suicide bomber, or car bomb. From the intel we've gathered, the aim is to destroy a large portion of Washington and London with nukes ... and maybe biologicals."

Baxter slid his chair back and pushed himself up from the chair. "We need to get help to Mack in Vienna."

"We've been trying to contact him all day," Nimesh said. "He's gone off-line, incommunicado."

"If that SOB is lucky enough to get out of this alive, I'll kill him."

CHAPTER 20

Bettina walked over to the kitchen counter, her legs numb. "I'm making coffee," she said to her reflection in the window.

"Make a large pot," Rainer said. He turned to Mack. "I have a list of questions."

Mack removed a business card from his pocket and dialed the number on the card. "Before it gets too late, I'll arrange for a ride back to Vienna in an hour." He inhaled the smell of the coffee brewing. "Hello Shah, it's Mr. John Wayne. Can you be back in Bad Vöslau in an hour and take us back to Vienna?"

"I am outside gate waiting for you to calling. I think you wanting ride to Vienna."

Mack put his hand over his phone. "He's outside the gate. What do you want to do?"

"I'll open the gate," Rainer said. "Tell him to pull just inside and wait until the gate closes before he drives up the driveway. We don't need anymore visitors."

Five minutes later, Shah was sitting at the kitchen table scarfing down cheese and drinking coffee.

Mack watched him with a fascination he couldn't describe. "You are a persistent piece of work, Shah. Remind me never to piss you off."

Shah swallowed his cheese and smiled politely. He didn't understand what Mack was saying. Siva translated in Persian. Shah smiled widely as he held up his coffee cup toasting himself.

Mack sketched out his plan. With the objective being to find and rescue Anna, he kept the detail to a minimum.

Rainer poured himself a second cup of coffee. He wasn't going to sleep tonight. He tried to punch holes in Mack's plan with little success, playing devil's advocate on every explanation Mack gave. Siva translated the debate for Shah.

Rainer finally capitulated after Mack repeatedly stressed the rescue of Anna was top priority.

Mack went back and forth whether to tell them about Karin. Knowing very little about her situation, he decided the time wasn't right.

Siva yawned, and instantly clamped her mouth shut as a shooting pain stung the swelling around her eye.

It was the signal to Mack to wrap things up. He handed Rainer back his Beretta M9 and went to hug

Bettina. She was already halfway to her bedroom. Siva and Shah shook hands with Rainer.

"Bettina needs to be alone," Rainer said walking them to Shah's car. He handed Mack the Glock. "Call me tomorrow when you are ready."

The drive back to Vienna went silent before the car exited the Bad Vöslau city limits. Siva dozed and the language difference between Mack and Shah made it difficult to hold a conversation. Both men were more comfortable in the silence.

As Shah's Volvo approached Siva's building, Mack told Shah to go home and rest. He wanted to check out Siva's apartment before he walked back to his hotel.

"I seeing you tomorrow before I go to base field," Shah said and drove off.

Standing outside the heavy wooden doors, Siva futilely dug through her purse searching for her keys.

Mack jingled her keys in front of her eyes. "I rescued these from Tariq Zarif."

Siva cringed at the mention of his name and rode the elevator fingering her swollen eye.

"You don't need to stay here tonight," Mack said.

"If I don't stay in my own apartment, they win."

He opened the apartment door to find the lights on and music playing. He held up his arm to stop Siva from entering.

Siva brushed his arm away as she entered. She dropped her purse on the end table.

Sensing Mack's unease, she said, "My cleaning lady came this afternoon. She always leaves the lights on and the radio playing. She believes it deters criminals."

Mack strolled around the apartment checking every room and closet, more for his own benefit. He closed and locked the sliding glass door to the balcony.

"Your place is clear so I will let you get your rest. Lock the door when I leave."

Siva moved close to Mack. "Please stay. I would feel so much more comfortable ... and safer."

It was still dark when the first flight of the day landed on the wet runway at Vienna International Airport. The private jet made a fast taxi to the last hanger and came to an abrupt stop near the doors of Sterling Silver, a private FBO, Fixed Base Operator.

J Otis Weil, the diminutive Chairman and Managing Partner of Sunden Capital bounded down the stairs of his Gulfstream 5. Behind him, a woman four inches taller pulled her headscarf forward just slightly and glided down the steps. J Otis offered his hand in assistance. She ignored him and strutted to the black Range Rover parked nearby. A devilish euphoria returned to J Otis. He liked a challenge. From the moment the plane left Washington, she'd shot down his persistent advances to join him in the plane's master bedroom.

Standing on the tarmac, he was mesmerized watching her step up into the Range Rover. He marched to the other side, jumped into the back seat and slammed the door.

Two Partners from Sunden Capital traveling with J Otis and Zoya Afari deplaned to see the Range Rover driving off. Looking around, a Mercedes E300 idled outside the front door of the FBO. The driver leaned against the car smoking a cigarette.

Both Partners lugged their bags over to the Mercedes. "Are you the car service?"

"Where to you going?" Shah asked.

"Hotel Imperial, do you know it?"

"Very much, yes. Is for you special deal. Two-hundred fifty Euro money, cash."

CHAPTER 21

On the second ring, Mack answered his phone by putting it on speaker. Siva came walking out of her bedroom barefoot having changed into faded blue jeans and a white Mozart T-shirt. Placing the phone on the coffee table, Mack held his finger to his lips.

"Strike two, Billy Mack," Baxter said with no intention to be humorous or ironic. "As a ballplayer you know what that means."

"Yes, sir." When in trouble, say as little as possible.

"Take me off speaker," Baxter demanded.

Mack took the phone off speaker and held it from his ear for Siva to hear.

"I have Ray Gunn, Nimesh and Jonah Klein on the phone. If you don't know Klein, you will soon. By the end of the day I'll be hiring him away from Nimesh and you may be working for him. You understand, right?"

"Yes, sir." When in trouble, say as little as possible.

"I'm turning this call over to Nimesh. He's scrubbed the intel you provided, has a good idea of what is transpiring and has some questions for you. Then we will talk about the next steps and what we want you to do. Are you ready?"

"Yes, sir." When in trouble, say as little as possible.

"Mack, Nimesh here. This is no time to be polite. If I'm wrong, interrupt me and correct me. That being said, what we've gleamed from both devices is telling but not complete. So, as I proceed with my briefing and I come to a hole needing to be filled, stop me if you have anything relevant."

"You don't need to worry about that."

"The USB devices contain visual evidence of Iran's nuclear program, specifically their uranium enrichment program. There is video of the Ayatollah and senior leaders touring the facility. What I find out of place is this group of Islamic religious leaders is being led by a woman. That doesn't happen in Iran."

Mack locked eyes with Siva. He put the phone back on speaker and said, "She is Zoya Afari, Siva's sister. Siva's here with me now."

"Really? What can she tell us about Zoya?"

Siva said, "She is now living in Vienna and

working at the IAEA. She has a doctorate in nuclear physics and is one of the leading experts in nucleosynthesis theory. She's a rocket scientist who knows how to make a nuclear bomb. Zoya worked at the Fordow nuclear facility until her marriage fell apart. She's separated from her husband and two daughters, awaiting divorce and unable to return to Iran." Siva inadvertently nodded, thinking of her two young nieces growing up without their mother.

"Does anyone have eyes on her?"

Siva pulled a small notebook from her purse, scribbled a quick note and held it up for Mack to read.

'She's on a business trip in Washington. Should be back today.'

"No," Mack replied. "Why?"

"Just curious." Nimesh went back to his summation. "In the video with the brutal murders of the two men pulled out of a Mosque, we've identified one victim, a Palestinian, as a Mossad agent. The second victim is not in any data bases."

Mack interrupted, "He was a Kurd engineer working at the Fordow nuclear facility. I don't have a name yet and why he was killed is a mystery. His hometown is Mahabad in the Kurdistan region of Iran." Mack felt it important to keep Shah's identity secret.

"How do you know this?"

Siva scribbled on her note pad, *FROM ME.*

"Siva heard a rumor from a contact in Tehran." Mack shrugged his shoulders.

"I'll pass that intel on to Susan to see if there is a hit in her data bases. The embedded code on the first device gives instructions on how to obtain and remove the nuclear materials already in Vienna and at the IAEA. A van has been secured as have ID badges and travel documents authorizing the transfer of nuclear waste. Not coincidentally, one of the world's greatest psychopaths, General Hafez Farid, is in Vienna and leading a group of Jahangir jihadists, Al Qaeda's hit squad funded by Iran. We believe the group's mission is to secure the nukes, get them out of Austria and into the US and UK without being detected."

"What's the status on the broken cross icon?" Mack asked. "Having three passwords is telling."

"Susan is running her algorithms and making some progress. It's her number one priority. She's never failed me yet. I've written a detailed summary of what we've discovered and sent it to your secure email address."

"Do we know the timing? Is there any-"

Nimesh interrupted, "Not yet and I don't think we'll know until the last minute. We've hacked into the server at the Atomic Energy Organization of Iran as well as Iran's top banks. As soon as any money is moved to accounts in the US or UK, we will know the attack is imminent."

"It would be better if we knew when the nukes are to be moved from the IAEA," Mack said. "Unfortunately, if we approach the Agency, they will deny any plot is afoot and the terrorists could get spooked and go underground."

Baxter cleared his throat. "Billy Mack, we have been authorized by the powers that be to stop the nukes from leaving Vienna ... by any means necessary."

"If that's the case, here's what I propose," Mack said. He relied on Siva's nods of reassurance as he explained his plan.

After the call, not a word was spoken for five minutes. Mack and Siva sat on the sofa looking out the sliding glass door at the lights of the *Prater* Ferris wheel off in the distance. Siva broke Mack's concentration and strolled into her bedroom leaving the door open. Chet Baker's saxophone began drifting out of the speakers in the ceiling. Siva walked out with a bottle of cognac in her hand.

The driver of the Range Rover left the airport, skirted the center of Vienna and stayed along the Danube. J Otis didn't pay attention to the route or even look out the windows. He was too busy working on his conquest of Zoya.

He was enthralled with her exotic look, dark beauty and self-assurance. Every time she rebuffed him, J Otis was more determined to bed her. He imagined her taking control and teaching him the erotic secrets of Persia.

The Range Rover approached the gate to the safe house and flashed its headlights twice. The tall iron gates opened and a young bearded man stepped out from behind a hedgerow holding a machine pistol. He waved the Range Rover through.

The safe house was a three-story villa clad with natural stonework fading from exposure to the sun. The wide front door was open in anticipation of their arrival. General Farid had ordered Hamid to open the front door and greet Zoya and her guest. Zoya walked past Hamid without a hint of recognition. J Otis smiled obligingly and nodded hello.

General Farid sat out on the back deck near the swimming pool watching the sunrise and smoking a Cuban cigar. It would be a cold day in Hell before he went to greet a woman. Zoya would come to him.

Zoya had long ago given up caring how Muslim men such as General Farid treated women. It was like beating your head against the brick wall and not expecting a headache. To him and his ilk, women were nothing more than objects to desire and own then exchange for a newer model once they've outlived their usefulness.

She marched out to the back porch, pulled a chair around to face the General and opened her briefcase. No pleasantries were exchanged.

General Farid's blood pressure spiked at the mere sight of Zoya. He would never admit it was jealousy. How a woman curried the favor of Iran's political and religious leaders was beyond his comprehension. Worse, Zoya Afari was a convert to Islam, married to the son of a wealthy, powerful and corrupt businessman and then one day decided to become a fervent supporter of Sharia. She couldn't be trusted ... and she was a *she*.

J Otis scurried around the other side of General Farid and pulled over a chair, keeping his distance. "Good to see you again, General."

General Farid blew cigar smoke toward J Otis.

Zoya placed a thick file folder on her lap and

removed a bundle of papers held together by a large black binder clip.

In perfect Persian, she said, "We commence operations at ten-o'clock tomorrow morning. The container from Fordow arrived yesterday and is now in the IAEA storage facility. All paperwork is in order and the money is being transferred to the various bank accounts later today. I have the transport papers for two shipments of nuclear waste from the IAEA storage facility on Brünnerstrasse. The delivery at the waste storage facility in Germany is scheduled for nine pm. By the time anyone realizes the shipment never arrived at its scheduled location, the cargo will be in London and on its way to Washington."

She handed the transport papers to the General. "Remember, the turn-off to the storage facility on Brünnerstrasse and the building itself are unmarked. The loading dock is around back. Go to Door No. 4. Hamid will do all the talking, as his German is fluent. Be careful with the cargo and do not open any container or you may be exposed to lethal doses of radiation. The route to the airport is marked on the map. Deliver the containers to the Sterling Silver hangars at VIA by eleven. It's the silver and red hangar near the far end of the airport."

She handed the General another bundle of papers. "These are the diplomatic immunity papers for entry into the US and UK. The documents are genuine, issued by the American State Department, thanks to J Otis. With these in hand, no one can check the cargo on the planes, no one." Zoya glared at General Farid until he acknowledged her.

She turned her attention to J Otis, speaking to
him in English. "Give him the ID badges."

J Otis handed the General four S&H security
badges and matching corporate identification cards.
"These are valid and are to be worn at all times on the
flight and upon arrival in Washington and London."

General Farid checked the head shot photos of
Tariq, Faruk, Hamid and Rez. He handed the ID card and
security badge belonging to Rez back to J Otis. "His
won't be used. Rez is no longer with us."

Zoya remained calm. Rez spoke fluent English
and could easily pass as an American. His task was to
work the diplomatic papers through customs in
Washington. "Where is Rez?"

The General puffed on his cigar. "I don't know.
He's been missing for a number of days. I can only
assume he lost his nerve and ran off. He's an Afghan so
you know he's a coward."

The glint in General Farid's eyes was telling. He
was sending her a message. Zoya wondered if he thought
Rez was her informant within the Jahangir. She also
wondered where he buried Rez's body. General Hafez
Farid was calculating and cold-blooded but he wasn't as
smart as he thought he was.

J Otis interrupted the staring contest. "There is no
time to make new IDs. Pick a replacement who looks like
the picture and I will make some calls."

"I will determine who replaces Rez," Zoya said,
keeping her eyes on General Farid. "Moving on ... Once
the cargo is delivered to the jets in the hangar, have one
of your men take the van to the designated parking spot,

wipe it clean and leave the money in the back."

J Otis quickly became bored. He stood up and perused the back porch looking for a wet bar. "Do you have anything to drink around here?"

General Farid ignored him.

"No alcohol is permitted in this house," Zoya said. She called for Hamid and asked him to make tea for J Otis.

"Where's the girl?" Zoya asked.

The General pointed subtly to the cellar.

The mention of a girl peaked J Otis's interest. He was no longer bored. "Girl? What girl?"

"I want to see her," Zoya said.

With his cigar jammed in the corner of his mouth, the General led Zoya and J Otis into the cellar.

The stale cellar air watered J Otis's eyes and he murmured something about making an important phone call as he climbed back up the stairs.

Anna lay in the fetal position against the bare cement wall, her eyes bloodshot and swollen from crying.

Zoya approached Anna like she was a wounded animal. She tenderly brushed the tangled hair from Anna's face and checked her arms and legs for any bruises or injuries. "Tariq was correct, she's perfect. We are taking her with us tomorrow."

General Farid lost his cool. "We are not taking her with us tomorrow. She will only be a distraction."

"How can such a little girl be a distraction? She does, however, provide assurance the American agent delivers me the device with the critically important lists. Americans are weak and do whatever it takes to save their children. My decision is final, the lists are too important."

The General dug his fingernails into his palms. "Getting the cargo into America and England is the only objective of this operation. Get these *lists* on your own time."

"Those lists provide the names of our operatives inside the US Government, including the White House. These agents are providing vital information. The other provides the names of traitors inside our country determined to help our enemies. These lists you so easily dismiss are critical to the security of Iran. The Supreme Leader has ordered the intelligence agencies to obtain them and bring them to him."

Zoya didn't like playing the Supreme Leader as her trump card but it kept General Farid in line. She walked over to Karin cowering in the corner.

"Who is this?"

"Her boyfriend is the American agent called Billy Mack. The one you say has the *lists*."

"She stays here. When I come back, I will decide what we do with her."

CHAPTER 22

As the sun crept into the apartment, Mack rolled off the sofa, slid open the sliding glass door and stepped out on the balcony. The fresh morning air cleared the remaining cobwebs from his brain. A dim glow in the eastern sky reddened the clouds, giving off an ominous vibe. Was it an omen of things to come?

He peeked into the master bedroom to check on Siva. She lay on her side with her back to the door. Feeling like a voyeur, he gently closed her bedroom door, left a cryptic note on the coffee table and headed back to his hotel.

Parked directly outside the entrance to Siva's apartment building was Shah's Volvo. He was nowhere in sight. Mack circled the car, pulled out his phone and Shah's card. He began punching in the number.

Shah came around the corner with a coffee in one hand and a baguette in the other. A cigarette dangled from his lips. "Mr. John Wayne," he said just loud enough not to disturb the neighbors. He placed his coffee on the Volvo, broke off the end of the baguette and offered it to Mack.

"Thanks," Mack said and bit off a piece of the warm bread. While he chewed, he perused the street unsure of what he expected to see.

"Not to worry," Shah said and lifted his shirttail to show his Colt Six-Shooter.

In a weird way the Six-Shooter comforted Mack and he blamed his restlessness on his fitful few hours of sleep.

Mack leaned against the dusty Volvo and bit off another chunk of bread. It was a waste of time to explain to Shah what he was to do at the Prater baseball field, even if it wasn't very complicated. He needed Siva to translate. He tapped the dial of his watch and raised eight fingers. "I will be back here at eight o'clock."

Back in his suite at the Imperial Hotel, Mack spoke with Nimesh and Susan. The Iranian Banks had just wired large amounts of dollars to a number of suspect accounts in Cyprus, Geneva, Singapore and Quetta, Pakistan. Susan was waiting to confirm transfers from these accounts to banks in the US and UK. As soon as he hung up, Mack stretched for twenty minutes, took a long, hot shower and studied the layout of the safe house from a collection of aerial photographs he'd received from Nimesh.

At ten minutes before eight o'clock, he opened the safe, pocketed the USB device and left the hotel. Across the street, he purchased a cheap phone for twenty Euros.

The Volvo was parked in the same spot in front of Siva's apartment and like earlier in the morning, there was no sign of Shah.

At Eight sharp, he buzzed the apartment for *Fr. S. Afari, 6 Stock,* checked the entryway and courtyard then rode the elevator up six floors. Siva opened the front door dressed in all black. Behind her, sitting around the dining table was Rainer, Bettina and Shah with a map of the *Prater* in front of them.

Shah waved Mack over. "I must soon leave, no."

"Siva, I need you to translate," Mack said as he crossed the floor. He spun the map around and got his bearings.

"The objective is for Shah to keep Tariq at the baseball field as long as possible while we steal our way into the safe house." Mack pushed the map closer to Shah. "Shoot him if you want."

Shah smiled and nodded.

"Shah, you come into the baseball field from left field." With his finger, he ran a path through left field. "If it is an ambush, the shooters will be hiding in the stands behind homeplate and won't have a direct shot. Walk to second base and face the stands. No matter what, don't leave second base." Mack pointed to second base on the map. "If it is a trap, you won't make it to second base."

"It will not be a trap. I know how Persian dogs

think," Shah said and Siva translated.

Mack hoped Shah was correct. "I expect Tariq's hunger for revenge will force him to come out on the field and talk to you. When he asks who you are and why you are there, give him this phone and this note and tell him I gave you two hundred Euros to deliver them to a man named Tariq. Before you give him the phone, ask him for identification and take your time reading over it. By this time you will know if Tariq came alone."

Mack handed Shah a folded sheet of paper and the cheap cellphone. "Only after you read his ID, then hand him the phone and note. While he reads the note, pull out your Six-shooter and do what you think is right. If there's a problem, I want you to walk away, back the way you came in."

Shah unfolded the note, saw it was written in English and handed it to Siva.

Siva read the note aloud. "*I am here and waiting for the call to confirm Anna is alive and at Staatsoper. Then I will show myself.*" Below the English words, she wrote the message in Persian script. She read the note aloud again, this time in Persian.

Mack said, "Bettina, make your presence outside the Staatsoper obvious and stay between the Ring Road and the entrance to the underground parking garage. If Anna is there, let them bring her to you." He handed Siva's phone to Bettina. "Keep this with you. We want the terrorists to think Siva is the one waiting for Anna."

Bettina handed her phone to Siva.

Mack added, "If Tariq shows up at the baseball field, we have one less terrorist to worry about at the safe house. If he doesn't, nothing's changed and we rescue Anna."

Mack placed an aerial photograph on top of the map. "This is the safe house. We don't have much information on the house. We can assume it is well guarded both inside and out."

"How do we get inside?" Siva asked.

"We storm the house creating the element of surprise," Rainer said. "Before anyone can react, we take out any guards we encounter and rush the house."

Shah cleared his throat to get attention and pointed to a spot left of the front gate. He spoke in Persian and Siva translated simultaneously. "During the day, one guard is always here by the front gate. He hides behind these hedges. During the night, the front gate is usually chained shut and two guards are always patrolling inside the perimeter. The house is very old and there are no cameras visible anywhere on the property."

He pointed to a small open space in the fence one hundred meters from the back of the house. "Right here there are three loose rods in the fence. You can slide the rods up, pull out the bottom and remove them. This is where you go in. The bushes and trees hide the hole in the fence. Follow the tree line and you can come to the house by the pool without being seen."

Mack was dumbfounded.

"How do you know this?" Siva asked.

"I spent some nights testing the security. These men are Jahangir. They kill well but they do not guard well."

"Have you seen inside the house?"

"I have been inside the house, but only the ground floor. There is not much on this floor."

"Do you have any idea where they might be keeping Anna?" Bettina asked.

"My guess would be she is in the cellar. Two windows on the North side of the house are frosted. When the lights are on, you can tell it is a large cellar."

Mack patted Shah on the back, impressed. "Time to get ready. Shah and Bettina leave in less than thirty minutes."

Rainer marched over to the closet next to the front door and dragged out a heavy duffel bag. He placed the bag on the floor by the sofa and began laying out a collection of military assault weapons on the sofa cushions. "I brought some tools to help us when we get to the safe house."

Mack looked over at Bettina for an explanation.

She smiled back at him as if to say, "*What the hell did you think he did for a living?*"

The trees near the *Prater* baseball field provided sufficient cover for Shah. He had a good vantage point of the field, the stands and the parking lots. Luckily, the entire *Prater* sports facility was a ghost town.

At nine-thirty he wedged his Colt six-shooter in his waistband at the small of his back, walked through the gate, crossed left field and stood where Mack pointed on the map, the place he called second base. Out of the corner of his eye he saw Tariq Zarif watching him from behind a green net.

Tariq circled around the green nets of the batting cage and entered the field next to the dugout. He strolled across the infield with his Steyr pistol in his right hand and hatred pumping through his arms and legs. When he saw it was Shah standing on second base, he aimed his pistol at Shah's chest.

Shah nervously raised the cheap cell phone and folded note.

"Who are you? Where is the American CIA assassin?"

Shah answered in heavily accented Persian. "An American gave me two hundred Euros to bring this phone and this note to this spot and give it to a man named Tariq."

"He sends a Kurd, the pigs of Persia," Tariq said and spit on the ground. "What did this American look like?"

Shah described Mack and lit a cigarette shaking like he was nervous.

Tariq gestured with his fingers for Shah to hand over the phone and note.

"The American said to only give these to Tariq Zarif. Please show me your identification."

Tariq stuck the pistol against Shah's head. "Here is my identification."

Shah handed over the phone and note and when Tariq read the note, he began his trek back through left field.

Tariq read the note twice and flipped open the phone. He turned on the phone and waited for the screen to come up. The phone was inoperative. It was a set up.

He saw Shah nearing the left field fence and fired a shot, missing high over his head. Shah hurried through the fence and disappeared behind the trees. Tariq sprinted after him and circled the thicket of trees. The Kurd was nowhere in sight as if he vanished into thin air.

He crumpled the note into a ball and threw it hard against the ground. Cupping his hands around his mouth, he screamed at the top of his lungs, "Fucking American coward."

J Otis arrived back at the safe house late and jumped out of the Range Rover before it came to a full stop. He stomped inside in search of General Farid. He found him sitting alone in a lounge chair on the back porch smoking his Cuban cigar.

J Otis stood over him. "I haven't received my payment for obtaining the paperwork granting diplomatic immunity. Until the money hits my account, there will be no diplomatic immunity and your cargo will be subject to customs inspection."

General Farid was more interested in the ringlets of smoke he was blowing over his head than responding to J Otis.

J Otis glared at the General.

Three smoke rings later, he said, "Talk to Zoya Afari."

J Otis strutted back into the house calling Zoya's name. Hamid pointed him up the stairs.

The mere presence of J Otis pissed off the General. Feeling sufficiently upset, he took it as a good sign to commence the operation. He liked being on edge. He tossed his half smoked cigar into the pool and called for Hamid.

"Have Tariq gather the troops so I can give the final orders. We are leaving at ten o'clock sharp."

Hamid had seen Tariq leave early in the morning without telling anyone where he was going and had not seen him return. "I will look for him," he said and walked away before any questions could be asked.

Standing outside in front of the house, Hamid cursed Tariq for caring only for his revenge. The General must be told Tariq had left again.

As if on cue, Tariq jogged up the driveway out of breath and sweating.

Hamid met him at the front door. "The General wants you to gather our brothers for final instructions."

Tariq lead the Jahangir into the mission room and closed the door. He wiped his forehead a number of times.

Wearing his sport coat and dress shirt, General Farid was dressed as a UN bureaucrat. "Why are you sweating Tariq? Are you nervous?"

"I was exercising so my muscles are ready for action."

Hamid opened a large box and handed out blue jumpsuits with 'IAEA' sewn into the left side of the chest and 'United Nations' sewn into the right side.

Tariq, Hamid and three other Jahangir donned the jumpsuits and clipped on their UN ID badges. General Farid inspected the men, walked them through the operational details one last time, having each man recite his responsibilities.

When he finished, he asked, "Where is Faruk?"

The Jahangir looked at each other. Tariq shrugged and zipped up his blue jumpsuit.

"Tariq?"

"It is not my day to watch him," Tariq answered mockingly, hoping for a few laughs.

Ignoring Tariq, the General pulled aside the three Jahangir not wearing jumpsuits. "After we leave, guard the grounds for thirty minutes then douse the entire house with the gasoline in the garage. Soak everything good then light up the house. Use all the gas so no evidence survives. The car for your escape is parked down the street. It is a blue Opel Astra. Walk, do not run to the car and meet us at the hangar. Samir, you are in charge." He handed Samir the car keys and left the Jahangir to themselves.

Zoya was not happy as she came down the steps followed by J Otis. She'd been listening to his monologue for twenty minute and had a headache. His demeanor on the other hand was the complete opposite. Zoya had showed him the wire transfer instructions and he was able to confirm the $5 million payment to his account. His focus switched from getting his money to getting Zoya.

Zoya lead him on, planning to use him until his private jet landed her back in Qom. "Bring the Range Rover to the front door," she said to J Otis, "and wait for me in the car."

Zoya found Tariq in the kitchen splashing water on his face. "Did you get the device from the American?"

Before Tariq could answer, General Farid walked

into the kitchen. He'd overheard Zoya.

"It is too late for these *lists* of yours," he said, enunciating 'lists' as if it were infected with ebola. "After the cargo is in the air, you can worry about the devices. Until then, we have an operation to complete. Tariq, get your men into the van."

Zoya said, "Not so fast. Tariq, bring up the girl from the basement and carry her to the Range Rover."

"The girl stays here. There will be no witnesses to this operation. That was a key operational directive."

Zoya stuck her finger in the General's face. "This is not your decision. The girl is critical to our cause. Go get her, Tariq."

General Farid fingered his sidearm as an obvious threat. "The girl stays here. We leave no witnesses."

CHAPTER 23

Siva drove Rainer's Audi A6 station wagon on the secondary roads taking a wide berth around the safe house. Mack and Rainer sat in the back seat preparing Rainer's military assault weapons. It wasn't the time to ask Rainer why he had such an arsenal — not until Anna was safe.

Rainer handed Mack an Ingram MAC-10 machine pistol, a Beretta M9 with a suppressor, a Sig Sauer P238 in an ankle holster and a serrated knife in a leather scabbard.

"The Beretta is your primary weapon. You're not trained on it so aim and shoot but make sure of your target and don't shoot if the target has Anna, she's close or you even see her." He handed Mack a second clip.

"Remember, use the MAC-10 pistol only if it's absolutely necessary. The other weapons I gave you are for close quarters."

Mack strapped on the ankle holster, lifted the shoulder strap for the MAC 10 over his head and adjusted it, then attached the scabbard to his belt.

Siva parked the Audi behind an empty store a half block north of the safe house. Mack and Rainer climbed out, put on full length overcoats and nodded to each other.

Rainer handed Siva a walkie-talkie. "Be ready to move when we call. If you're in any danger there is a Glock in the cubby by your elbow. Just point and shoot."

Siva only nodded. She had trouble speaking, knowing her sister was likely in the house.

Mack recognized the look. He said, "The objective is to take Zoya alive but Anna's rescue comes first."

Siva nodded again and looked away.

Nearing the back fence of the safe house, Rainer said, "Remember what I said Mack, don't shoot unless you can identify the target. I don't want to be digging your bullet out of my ass."

Rainer arrived first at the small entry point in the fence, the spot Shah pointed out. The poles in the fence were already removed. He silently gestured to Mack with a shrug of his shoulders. Mack crawled through and crouched behind the thick bushes. He discarded his overcoat and pushed it into the bushes. Rainer followed suit and pointed to the direction he would be heading — wide right around the perimeter to the front of the house.

Mack gestured to the tree line left of the house. He was to follow the line until he reached the house. His senses were on high alert, infinitely more acute then when he played baseball. Standing at home plate with the eyes of fifty-thousand fans on you as you waited for a pitch was a walk in the park compared to what he was feeling at this moment. As he crept along the tree line he was more focused then he'd ever been in any game, or at any time in his life.

On the other side of the property, he heard a 'pfffft' followed by low grunt and the rustling of bushes. He prayed it was Rainer's silenced Beretta he'd just heard. Mack moved deliberately inside the tree line. At the corner of the house, he kept low and jogged across a small open area to the side of the house. He surveyed the pool and back deck. The area was empty. He crept along the wall and peeked around the corner to the back porch. The sliding glass door into the house was partially open. He stared at the opening.

"Gotta do what you gotta do," he whispered as he sprinted along the pool to the sliding glass door with the Beretta pointing the way. He didn't stop until he was inside the house with his back against the wall. His eyes, nose and throat started to burn. The overpowering stench of gasoline filled the house. He turned the corner and ran through the large living area toward the front door holding his breath.

Passing the kitchen, he heard muffled coughs behind a door. He twisted the gasoline-soaked door handle and pushed the door. The scratchy voice cried out, "*Hilfe, hilfe.*" Her voice becoming louder, clearer, hopeful.

He took the steps two at a time. In the corner, Karin was lying on the cement floor trying to breathe, her skin a heavy pink. The floor was soaked in gasoline.

"Karin, where's the girl?" Mack asked.

"They took her."

He untied her feet and hands and picked her up. He ignored her screams of pain as he climbed the steps. Outside the kitchen, he looked left and right for the fastest way outside. He started for the front door and stopped.

Stepping into the doorway with a lighter in his hand was a clean-shaven Jahangir dressed like an American college student. Mack recognized the face.

"You don't need to do this Samir."

Samir lifted the lighter. "Give me the USB device and I will let you both go."

"Tell me where the young girl is," Mack replied trying to buy time.

Samir stepped back and lit the lighter. "Last chance."

"Let me bring her outside first."

Samir held out his free hand. "Throw me the device and I-" Samir's eyes seemed to pop out of his head a split second before his forehead exploded and blood spattered against the open front door. He dropped the lighter on the gasoline soaked rug inside the door.

Mack sprinted with Karin still over his shoulder, stepping on Samir's dead body lying across the threshold. He took three long steps onto the grass, dropped Karin and fell on top of her. Wrapping his arms around her he rolled away from the house until she pushed him off.

Rainer grabbed Karin's arms and pulled her further down the yard. Mack crab walked after her as the house exploded into one large fireball blowing out the windows.

For a split second it was as if the world stopped spinning. Then a swoosh sucked the air back into the heat, pulling Mack toward the house. He clamped his hands into the grass digging his fingers into the dirt, hanging on for dear life.

Rainer lifted Karin, carried her to the Koi pond near the garden and dunked her in the water. She screamed in pain until her skin stopped burning.

"Where is Anna, the young girl?" Rainer asked.

"They took her. The woman in charge demanded it and was very happy when the one called Tariq carried her away."

It was as if all the blood and oxygen was sucked out of Rainer.

"We'll find her," Mack said and lifted his walkie-talkie. He called Siva, giving her instructions where to pick them up.

"How?" Rainer yelled.

"Nimesh or Susan should have learned something useful. If not, we do whatever it takes including trading the device."

Rainer dropped to his knees, scooped up water with his hands and splashed his face. "We move to the street as you talk to your people. I shot two sentries before I rushed the door. There may be more around."

"Good call," Mack said. "Siva should be at the gate." He lifted Karin out of the water.

"I can walk," she said.

At the front entrance, they pulled open the double gate as two fire engines arrived with sirens blaring and blue lights flashing. The trucks flew up the driveway honking.

Rainer collected Mack's weapons and hid them behind a bush. "If the police arrive before Siva, there is no need for them to see these."

Siva arrived just as Mack's call connected with Nimesh and Susan. Rainer retrieved the weapons and hid them inside the wheel well in the back end of the Audi.

Karin heard the police sirens getting closer. She sat on the curb. "I should go to hospital."

Rainer glared at Mack and imperceptibly shook his head no.

Karin said, "Go find the girl, her name is Anna. I will tell the police what happened to me. I will not tell them about you."

Siva drove away with Mack and Rainer sitting in the back seat. Rainer was checking the weapons and fighting to stay calm. Only his Beretta M9 had fired and he re-loaded the clip.

"Tell me something good Nimesh," Mack said into his phone. "We have a little girl in deep trouble."

CHAPTER 24

After crossing the Danube River in heavy traffic, Siva exited the Audi on the first turnoff. Rainer was busy staring out the window thinking of Anna. Mack was deep in conversation with Nimesh and Susan trying to put the pieces of the jigsaw together and figure out where Anna, Zoya, General Farid, the Jahangir and the nukes were headed. For Mack it was like putting together a jigsaw puzzle called *Blue Sky*.

Siva let the car roll to a stop on the shoulder. "Where are we going?" she asked, frustrated.

Mack concentrated on his phone conversation. "The transport of nuclear material limits the options," Mack said after hearing Nimesh and Susan's assessment and analysis of the intel. Try as he might, no firm, logical conclusions could be drawn from the intelligence they had.

Nimesh said, "These are suitcase nukes. The mass of uranium is no more than fifteen kilotons, about the size of a basketball. The type of transport is only important if neutron sensors are in use. This restricts rail transport, too many sensors. Air travel to major airports would be difficult. That leaves ground transport and shipping."

Susan cut in when Nimesh paused, "The money transfers from the Iranian banks are complete. The accounts in the US and UK have received the wire transfers and the money has been withdrawn from the banks. This means the nukes are likely to be transported by air, at least to the US. We have accessed the systems for every airline flying to and from Vienna, looking at manifests for both commercial and cargo aircraft. We have nothing associated with the UN or IAEA."

"Keep digging and call when you have anything new, I don't care how negligible it is." Mack leaned back and closed his eyes. What's missing? He ran through the options. The nukes can be either carried out, driven out, shipped out, railed out or flown out.

During his baseball career, Mack suffered a slump every season, as all players did at least once a season. When he went into a slump, he went back to fundamentals, quit over-thinking and simplified his swing and his game. It was time to do that now.

If the terror attack is imminent, General Farid and the Jahangir are not going to worry about neutron sensors. By the time the authorities react to the sensors, the suitcase nukes will be long gone. He called Nimesh back. "The uranium was shipped from Iran under the guise of nuclear waste to be analyzed by the IAEA, a bureaucracy. That means paperwork. Can you trace the system for a shipment?"

"I'll get Jonah Klein on it." Mack listened to Nimesh walk down the hall to Jonah's office and explain Mack's request.

In two minutes, Jonah said, "I'm in the IAEA's system. What am I looking for?"

"Shipments from Iran."

Jonah hummed as he typed. "There's nothing here, no shipments to or from Iran. I find references to Iran listed as country of origin in four storage records with authorization from a company called Schwike & Hoffman, but no reference to any nuclear material."

"Did you say Schwike & Hoffman?"

"Yes, they provide security for IAEA's nuclear storage."

Mack recalled the S&H website he'd analyzed. "S&H also leases private jets. Have any of the company's jets filed a flight plan?"

"Three flight plans are filed. The first is for a flight to Istanbul at midday. The plane is owned by S&H and leased to Sunden Capital. The other two flight plans are filed for Reykjavik, Iceland and Antwerp, Belgium. The departure times are twelve-o-five and twelve-ten. Both planes are leased by the same company, Wiener Computer Logistics."

"Anything to the US or UK in the next twenty-four hours? Are there any UN connections?"

"Nothing on the UN. You know flight plan destinations are not always final. Flight plans can be changed while an aircraft is in the air. I'll arrange for alerts to be sent to my computer if there is a change to any flight plans."

"Thank you Jonah, you too Nimesh."

Mack massaged his temples with a circular motion. It was too coincidental. He'd found what was missing.

"I know where the nukes are going and I bet Anna is there."

J Otis couldn't take her ignoring him any longer. Zoya was paying attention to the girl and not him. He had important information to impart to her. He started talking, raising his voice each time Zoya said something to Anna. Even if Zoya wasn't listening to him, he wasn't going to be deterred. She was going to hear what he had to say.

"I've made significant market bets, shorting the market indices and buying defense stocks. I'm going to make a killing as soon as you detonate, no pun intended. If you want, I can cut you in for a piece. You know, I scratch your back, you scratch mine." J Otis was speaking literally. "I'm talking eight zeros here, hundreds of millions of dollars. We can do a lot of scratching."

"We will talk on the flight to Qom," Zoya said. "Now is not the time."

"Qom? We are flying to Istanbul first. I have two days of business to complete before I take you to Tehran, not Qom."

"The plans have changed. We are flying to Qom directly. I have precious cargo to protect."

J Otis said, "I pulled the right diplomatic strings, I financed a good portion of this operation and used my company's assets. I'm not changing my plans."

"I will make it worth your while."

"Now we're getting somewhere."

CHAPTER 25

"Head to the airport" Mack said. "There's an FBO at the airport called Sterling Silver. S&H owns the company and provides security for Sterling Silver as well as Vienna International Airport. S&H also owns a jet leasing company based out of Sterling Silver's operations. This is how General Farid is getting the nukes out of Austria."

"I hope you're right, we only have one shot to get my daughter."

"A couple of days ago an *employee* of Wiener Computer Logistics tried to con his way into my hotel room while I was out. It's way too coincidental."

Rainer reached back to collect the Beretta M9s,

the Sig Sauer P238s and serrated knives. "With Anna inside no machine pistols will be used, it's too dangerous." He handed the Beretta M9 back to Mack. "Be careful."

"How are we going in?" Mack asked.

"We each have something the other wants," Rainer said. "Give me five minutes to find the proper position then you and Siva make yourselves visible, show them the device if you have to. Just keep the General distracted until I can neutralize him and the Jahangir. Zoya will then take charge and gladly make the exchange. After Anna's safe, you do what you have to do."

Creeping the Audi up to the airport service building next to the Sterling Silver complex, the atmosphere inside the car was potent, full of aggression. Mack gauged Siva. She was examining a Glock 9 like she'd been fully trained to handle the weapon. She pulled back the slide, chambered a round from the magazine and checked the sight.

Rainer secured his weapons. What he was doing was second nature and Mack wanted to ask him why but knew better. Rainer was in no mood to talk. Walking away, Rainer held up five fingers indicating the number of minutes he needed to get in place and disappeared behind the service building.

"He's a pro," Siva said as she and Mack waited the prescribed amount of time then marched across the parking lot and through Sterling Silver's glass front doors. The lobby was empty, cold and ghostly quiet. Mack led the way through the door behind the ticket counter and into the back offices. He opened the door marked

Training Room. Four bodies, a pilot, two women and an S&H security guard were lying in the middle of the floor with blood pooling around each head. Mack closed the door before Siva could look in. He guided Siva out the back door and headed toward the hangars.

Walking across the tarmac, the sun peeked out of the clouds and warmed the air. Siva stopped next to a Dassault Falcon and grabbed Mack's arm. "Give me the device."

"What? Why?"

"Because you're more likely to get shot than I am. If I have the device, I can still trade it for Anna. Isn't that what matters?"

"Not going to happen. It's too dangerous."

Mack marched the last thirty meters of tarmac and stood in the open hangar door waiting to be noticed. He'd lost sight of Siva.

Men wearing blue jumpsuits were loading the nukes in two separate Gulfstream 5 jets. General Farid wore a sport coat and looked like the office manager. He came around the white van and like a good soldier already had his sidearm out and pointed at Mack. Siva stepped from behind the hangar door and stood next to Mack, shoulder to shoulder.

Seeing Mack at the hangar door, Tariq shoved the wooden crate he was loading into the cargo bay and snatched his AK 47 off the cargo bay floor. He sprinted toward Mack raising the rifle.

With the butt of the rifle against his chest, Tariq stopped suddenly and smiled like Satan about to collect another soul. He raised the gun to his shoulder and took aim. Revenge was sweet.

There was no sound as blood began to soak through the center of Tariq's shirt. He looked down, dropped the AK 47 and fell to his knees. He touched his chest and examined the blood on his hand. He looked up to the sky, teetered and fell face first on cement floor.

Mack stole a look around to see where Rainer was hiding.

In the commotion, General Farid moved behind the Range Rover for protection while urgently trying to locate the shooter. Zoya lowered herself in the back seat and held on tightly to Anna. J Otis was on the Range Rover's floorboard rocking back and forth with his knees in his chest. Hamid and the two remaining Jahangir finished loading the wooden crates onto the two planes, unconcerned about being shot.

Zoya powered down the window and yelled out, "You want this beautiful girl and I want the list of names of the traitors to my country. It should be an easy decision."

Mack replied, "Release the girl first. Then we-"

His heart dropped into his stomach as he felt a cold steel gun barrel pressed against his temple. He drifted his eyes over to Siva holding the Glock. Her coffee brown eyes deliberated, deciding what to do.

"Give me the device," Siva demanded, her voice rigid, cold.

CHAPTER 26

Mack stood stock still knowing any false move would probably end his and Anna's lives. The indifference in Siva's eyes chilled him to the bone. He'd been duped and didn't see it coming.

Siva pushed the gun hard against his temple, reached into his front pocket and took out the USB device. She held it up for Zoya to see. "I meet Anna halfway and when she is released I give you this."

Rainer emerged from behind a two-story metal storage rack of airplane parts and supplies, his Beretta pointed at Siva.

Siva said, "Rainer, don't shoot. I won't hand the device over until Anna is out of danger." As a calming gesture, she put the Glock into her waistband at the small of her back.

Rainer slid his aim over to the Range Rover. J Otis had crawled out of the far side and was running toward the emergency exit. Rainer fired two suppressed shots into the door above him. J Otis dropped and splayed out face first on the cement floor, then covered his head with his arms.

Zoya stepped out of the backseat and helped Anna down, keeping her in front as a human shield. She pulled down Anna's sundress and held her firmly by the shoulders until Siva was halfway. When Siva stopped twenty meters away, Zoya let go. Anna ran to Siva and hugged her. Siva kept her cold, emotionless expression as she wrapped her arms around Anna. She released her grip and told Anna to run to her father.

Siva remained where she was until Anna and Rainer were out on the tarmac. She approached Zoya, removed the Glock from the small of her back.

"It should never have come to this," Siva said, with a sorrowful tone.

General Farid came around from behind the Range Rover with his service pistol hanging in his hand. Over his right shoulder, Hamid stood with his feet apart aiming his AK 47 at Mack, just in case.

The General holstered his service pistol as he sauntered over to Mack. It was a victory walk. He held out his hand and motioned with his fingers for Mack to give him the Beretta.

Mack slapped his pistol into General Farid's hand. The General raised the pistol and pried the barrel into Mack's mouth. A playful look suddenly washed over his face. He was enjoying himself. His eyes unexpectedly widened and he jerked the pistol out of Mack's mouth. "Don't go anywhere," he said then strolled over to Siva and Zoya.

"This is what happens when women think they are as strong as men. Operations fall apart and people die. You should stick to your natural duties, sex, cooking and cleaning. That is what nature intended."

Siva turned to respond.

General Farid fired Mack's Beretta, hitting Siva in the chest.

Zoya screamed as Siva fell into her arms. Her body's inertia pulled Zoya down with her.

The General aimed and shot Zoya in the temple.

"Hamid, instruct the pilots to move the airplanes out to the tarmac and prepare for takeoff."

General Farid strolled over to Mack determining how he would humiliate him before he killed him. He was enjoying himself thinking of how he would kill Mack. It had to be a form of humiliation that would haunt the American assassin while he burned in hell with the Jews, the Christians and the other pigs. He tossed Mack's Beretta on Siva's body and began ranting about the Great Satan would be destroyed.

The roar of the jet engines at the other end of the hangar had drowned out his words. He kept talking and circling Mack until the planes were out on the tarmac.

"When the investigation is over, Billy Mack will be the killer of record, if Billy Mack is your real name. I am going to be very generous and kill you quickly. But first, tell me your real name so I can tell the Ayatollah of the famous CIA assassin I killed to retrieve the lists that save the Islamic Republic and the coming Caliphate. The story of General Hafez Farid will be legendary." The General came nose to nose with Mack. "I am doing you a favor. Your death will save you from seeing the humiliating defeat Islam and Allah are about to inflict on your country and the world."

Mack was not going to give him the satisfaction of a direct response. "How did Tariq have this photo of me from Chicago?" His voice was inquisitive as if they were having an everyday conversation.

"I took it off your fellow agent before I killed him. Walters, I think his name was."

Mack handed the photo to the General. "I want you to have this on your person when I kill you."

The General moved closer. He was a master at intimidation. "Okay, we are done. Tell me your real name so you can die in peace."

Mack looked hard into General Farid's eyes. "My name is William McMillan and *I* always win."

Coming from the Tarmac, two gunshots echoed through the hangar. A piercing screech followed by a loud clanging rattled the planes before the engine noise dissipated. Both Gulfstream V jets puttered to a full stop, smoke rising from the rear engines. Two more shots hit tires. Air hissed out of the tires as the planes listed to the right.

Out of the sun and through the hangar door came a silhouette dressed as a traditional Kurdish warrior and a red and white *Shemagh* wrapped around his head.

General Farid laughed loudly as the old man's face became visible. He raised his service pistol.

Fifty yards out, Shah fired his Colt Six-Shooter knocking the General's pistol out of his hand.

Mack sprinted over, slid across the floor kicking the gun away. He pushed himself to his feet, spun around and kicked the General in the jaw with his right heel.

Dazed by the kick, the General spun his head back to the left to see Shah strolling toward him. Before he could react, Shah had the barrel of the Colt against the General's forehead. General Hafez Farid peed his pants.

Shah pulled the trigger. "That was for my son," he said in Kurdish. "Burn in hell."

Shah ignored Mack and hurried to Siva. She was able to push herself up and was lying with her back against her sister with her right hand over her chest, blood seeping slowly through her fingers. Shah bent down, removed Siva's hand and checked the wound. He pressed his handkerchief on the bullet hole and placed her hand on top. "Push until you have pain then ease off only a little."

Mack's emotions were like a pinball inside his head. Shah was calmly attending to Siva, making her comfortable and he didn't know whether to help or walk away.

"Come to here, Mr. John Wayne. She need you to helping."

A black Mercedes SUV came to a screeching halt just outside the hangar. Casey Ryan and two CIA cover agents surveyed the scene. The agents spoke into their shoulder-mounted walkie-talkies. An unmarked BMW

X5s with the windows tinted black came to a screeching halt. Four muscular men in black tactical gear and vests with COBRA in block letter across the chest emerged.

Rainer and Anna walked up to the Cobras. Rainer spoke quietly with the Cobra commander, left Anna with the Cobras and jogged across the hangar. He bent down and hugged Siva, thanking her.

Mack looked at him like he was crazy. "What the hell?"

Rainer held up the USB device. "Siva put it in the pocket of Anna's dress."

Siva sat up, moaned in pain, then grimaced and laughed. "Baseball and Taekwondo?" she asked.

"Gotta do whatcha gotta do."

Siva looked at him strangely.

EPILOGUE

Shah steered the old Volvo up the busy *Mariahilfer Strasse*, the main shopping street for locals in Vienna. He was in no hurry, enjoying the hustle of the big city.

"I happy Siva is to be okay."

"Me too," Mack said. "She was very lucky."

"The *Malaa'ika* ... you say them ... *Angels*, were looking to her."

Siva spent three hours on the operating table to remove the slug she took from General Farid. The doctor had no explanation for the strange path of the bullet but no internal organs were damaged. She had never seen anything like it. Mack and Shah spent the last hour at her bedside before the doctor chased them away so Siva could rest.

"Turn right at the next street," Mack said.

Two young girls wearing short skirts and loose blouses took their time in the crosswalk. "You not see such womens in my country," Shah said matter-of-factly.

"Are you returning to Kurdistan?" Mack asked, staring out at the oncoming traffic.

"I am not knowing," Shah replied and tapped his chest with his index finger. "There is no Kurdistan country, only Kurdistan soul. Beside, I having no more family for me in Mahabad. Maybe I stay and driving taxi here, is more safe than Iran."

"Rainer will be happy."

"Mr. Rainer is special man. He is number one Kripo for government of Austria." He winked at Mack. "I am only thinking so, not knowing."

For the remainder of the drive they rode in comfortable silence through the morning traffic.

Parked outside the steel and glass office building housing BIG's lawyers, Mack and Shah shook hands, each squeezing firmly, knowing it was likely the last time.

Mack gave Shah his card and wrote his personal cell phone number on it. "Call me anytime, for anything."

"Okay, Mr. John Wayne. I calling." Shah smiled resolutely, ready to face a new city and new life. He eased down on the gas pedal and turned the Volvo into a gap in traffic.

Mack spent the rest of the day cooped up in a conference room with teams of lawyers representing the various *stakeholders*, a term bandied about by the lawyers to give their clients more importance. By late afternoon, there was only one issue remaining before the final purchase agreement could be signed. BIG was requiring S&H to indemnify against any harm or loss from all S&H actions taken prior to the date of the acquisition, a standard clause.

The lawyers for S&H and Sunden Capital were holding fast to their position on indemnification: there would be none.

Final decision.

Mack thought of Siva lying in hospital bed and Shah starting over in a strange new city. He knew what was more important.

Priorities.

He stood, raised his hands and garnered the attention of everyone sitting around the long table.

"We have only one issue left to resolve and we seem to have come to an impasse. I have the solution." He let the words hang in the air.

"S&H and Sunden Capital will fully indemnify BIG and it's subsidiaries for any harm or loss on any and all actions occurring prior to the date on the purchase agreement. If Sunden Capital and S&H are not willing to provide such an indemnification, the deal is off. I'm done negotiating."

Mack packed his briefcase and marched out the door. As soon as the conference room door closed behind him, a roar erupted throughout the room rattling the door.

Standing on the sidewalk letting the sun warm his face, he half expected Shah to drive up and ask if he was *wanting ride*. He found himself *wanting ride*, hoping Shah would pull up in the old Volvo.

Instead, he felt someone approaching rapidly from behind.

The partner from Sunden Capital stuck his nose in Mack's face. His skin was crimson with irritation and his blonde hair appeared to be white. "You don't walk away from a deal with J Otis Weil and Sunden Capital," he said in a voice that was at the same time measured and menacing. "It's not good for your health."

"Why didn't you pose in any of the pictures at the private equity conference in Chicago?" Mack asked.

"What?"

Mack lifted his phone and clicked a picture.

"What the fuck are you doing? Delete that picture."

After sitting with Siva for two hours, Mack walked into the Hotel Imperial to see the concierge desk empty. He inquired at the front desk and was told Karin was on medical leave. No other information would be provided.

Standing on the balcony off his room he looked across the city to the red gondolas on the *Prater* Ferris wheel. He couldn't delay the call any longer.

"Hello Rose, is Mr. Baxter in?"

"Yes, I'll connect you Mr. Mc ... Billy Mack."

The call went much better than expected. Baxter and Gunn were fully supportive of his decision to walk away from the S&H acquisition. No deal was better than the wrong deal.

"I've received repeated calls from J Otis Weil," Baxter said. "He's threatening to sue you, me, Ray and the firm. He demanded I pass a message on to you. Here it is and I quote, 'J Otis doesn't get mad he gets even.'"

"Did he really refer to himself in the third person?" Mack asked with a laugh.

A week later, Mack wheeled Siva out the front door of the hospital. Outside the main entrance, Rainer and Anna leaned against a black BMW X5 with its windows blacked out and its back door wide open.

On the drive through Vienna, Anna peppered Siva with questions on how it felt to get shot and whether she died and came back to life. Siva happily answered each question.

Inside her apartment building, Siva endured the painful rattle of the old elevator as it ascended. Try as she might, she could not hide her pain.

Mack opened the door, let Siva into the apartment and followed her to the table near the kitchen area. Standing in the middle of the table was a framed picture of Shah, his wife and his son standing in the courtyard of a freshly whitewashed house with proud smiles on their faces, paintbrushes in their hands and the green and brown Zagros Mountains behind them.

There was a note for Siva written on the photo:

Take care of Mr. John Wayne

JOHNNY

ABOUT THE AUTHOR

Johnny is a former banker, restaurant owner, defense industry analyst and for one summer, a band manager. His first job was hustling programs and scorecards at Minnesota Twins games when he was 12 years old. He quickly learned it was not a career he would pursue.

CPSIA information can be obtained at www.ICGtesting.com
Printed in the USA
LVOW08s0113030516

486389LV00001B/43/P